# CHINAMANS BLUFF

CHRISTOPHER MALINGER

www.christophermalinger.com

**Cover design by Polar Photography**

www.polarphotography.com

ISBN: 13-978-0-9907018-9-7 ISBN: 10-9907018-9-1

*To Nicole*

# INTRODUCTION

"Well—let's leave it to Chance, whose ally is Time that
cannot be hurried, and whose enemy is Death, that will not wait."
Joseph Conrad

# PROLOGUE

Nestled between the sandstone cliffs of the Paleozoic Plateau is Chandlers Bend, Wisconsin. If the Native Americans had a name for the location, it was compressed under the weight of economic progress. A railroad juncture born out of geology rather than design, it was the juxtaposition of latitude and longitude, bound by baselines, secured by benchmarks, and knitted together with the steel and ties of the railroads. This coincidental crisscrossing of commerce created an opportunity for Jacob Chandler and his partner Samuel Beck. Accepting the challenge to feed the railroad's insatiable hunger for firewood, both men willingly obliged and created a fueling station at this intersection of fate.

Originally christened Chandler's Camp by the railroad men, subsequently, it became Camp Chandler. Over time, people complained it reminded them of a military outpost more than a town. Eventually, the *Camp* prefix was dropped, and *Bend* added, soothing most protests.

The history books speak glowingly of the founders Jacob and Samuel but only briefly mention the young girl who accompanied them. The narrative of her life consisted of an ambiguous line, "... accompanying them was a young girl." And just as unexplained was her departure. Unidentified, in the account, her role, being left to speculative gossip, became a pastime, ingrained into the soul of Chandlers Bend's future inhabitants.

Like any confluence of trade, people began to settle and build their lives—its foundation, nothing more than a whiskey wagon. Later, women would come to provide comfort and release after the backbreaking work of the railroad workers. They were a mixture of roustabouts, drifters, and ruffians who heaved together in a continual chorus of "Huh!" as they pulled on their lining bars, shuffling along the surveyor's predetermined path.

With the rails came the settlers. And with all this convergence of humanity, souls needed saving. The Methodist church was the first to be erected and built near the crossroads. Presumably, it well situated for catching souls before they strayed too far into the temptations of camp life. Soon after, the Catholics built their church on a ridge on the opposite side of the tracks. Its elevated height, perhaps, made the parishioners feel closer to God.

Almost simultaneously, a dance palace coexisted on top of a nearby bluff to lift the growing community's spirits in other ways. Using a series of switchback staircases, it exceeded the Catholic Church's elevation, leaving one to ponder if altitude increased one's salvation. For, many a soul went up those dancehall stairs, and many a story descended—but a town without tales ceases to survive.

# 1
---

Mingled with the footfalls below him, he heard their hostile calls, coupled with the barking and yelping of dogs who charged through the dry underbrush. Surrounded by his pursuers, he prayed they would, somehow, fail to see him.

Lying motionless on a Wisconsin sandstone bluff, beneath the day's swelter of an arid June sky, he breathed heavily. He considered the incessant hammering of his heart a giveaway as it pounded in his chest. His ears ached from the throbbing pressure, and he feared they were going to burst. His gulps for air stirred the soil under his face and clung to his lips and tongue. He spit the sand from his mouth, only to have more rise in defiance of his efforts. His torn and sweaty clothing clung to his body, but he dared not raise his head. He wanted the ground to open up and devour him, becoming one with Chinamans Bluff.

Louis Girard's barbershop was the hub of debate in Chandlers Bend. It became the United States Senate, the English Houses of

Parliament, and the Russian Duma. So, it was a forgone conclusion at the local town hall assemblies that all outcomes were determined at the barbershop. The town meetings had become nothing more than a rubber stamp on the preordained conclusion.

In its smoke-filled chamber and hair-strewn floor, The Great War was refought, illnesses diagnosed, the depressed economy debated, and the latest domestic tittle-tattle—were all fodder for discussion. At times, the exchange became heated, boiling over to near fisticuffs.

"*Couper la poire en deux,* let's cut ze pair in half," Louis would say to restore peace. His appeal for civility would calm the combatants, and an uneasy truce would reign. Other times, when adversaries happened to seek his services at the same time, an uncomfortable silence hung in the air like a blacksmith's hammer, ready to pound flat any effort at dialogue. For the most part, this was a rarity, but hurt feelings and perceived injustices remained, unforgiven even to their placement in the local cemetery.

Like most of the inhabitants of Chandlers Bend, Louis Girard came from someplace else. And luck, that fickle coin of chance, played a big part in that decision. If one ventured to ask why anyone settled in this crossroads of fate, few could give an honest answer.

The town's impressive bluffs could capture a visitor's attention for a brief time, but beyond a week, they felt more like walls. They blocked the stunning comings and goings of the daily sun, depriving the inhabitants of the joy that others enjoyed outside these confinements. Absent, too, were picturesque brooks or rivers to idle away a day spent fishing or swimming. No, Chandlers Bend simply became an X on the map—the interlacement of two railroads, further split by one state highway. Those who felt obliged to stay either lacked the good sense to leave or the resources to do so.

Louis arrived in town by way of the railroad. A short, rotund man, he carried himself with dignity, befitting what one could call an air of refinement. His stately persona added inches to his stature. He checked into the Bluff Side Hotel, intent on catching the intersecting train bound for St. Paul. Like all of the wanderers trapped in Chandlers Bend awaiting passage to someplace else, he chose the hotel's restaurant for its source of nourishment and conversation.

The Bluff Side Hotel, a mediocre remnant of its former glory, now only two stories high with a twelve-room capacity, was all that Felix and Beatrice Williamson could afford to rebuild after the *Great Fire of 1917*. Although it was not of the magnitude of the Peshtigo Fire or the Great Chicago Fire, it was a hardship for many of its inhabitants. The fire's origin, attributed to careless soldiers and their ruckus behavior at the town's dancehall, proved to be an enormous financial setback for many of the town's inhabitants, and the use of the word *great* matched its effect on their lives.

Mrs. Beatrice Williamson, a sturdy woman of remarkable fortitude, approached Louis' table. She scanned the fragments of his croquette of minced chicken, mashed potatoes, and a pool of beet juice. "I trust you had an enjoyable meal, sir?" She asked politely.

"*Houte cuisine, madam*," he said.

She gave him a curious stare. "Oh," she uttered, appearing wounded by his remark.

"Oh no, madam, *pardon*, I appear to have upset you. Your meal was *magnifique*, or as you American's say, 'fit for zee king.'"

Beatrice beamed with delight and turned a shade of pink. Magic took place in that brief exchange that can only be described as fate. Flattered by his recovered compliment, she said contritely, "That will be thirty-five cents, sir." Then, as if to minimize the charge after such a glowing review, she added, "Of course, that includes a slice of cherry pie."

"*Ouï, madame, mon préféré.*"

In a trancelike state, she hurried off to the kitchen.

Now Beatrice was ripe for romance. She steadfastly clung to the name of Mrs. Williamson out of status for her late husband, Felix— an early settler in Chandlers Bend. She also used the title as a foil against unwanted advances by uncouth locals. Felix died during the Great Influenza outbreak. She thought it a cruel joke for him to have survived the war only to be killed by some unseen microbe. The loss of the first hotel, followed by her husband's death, galvanized her against the trials she would face in the years to come. Fearless in her pursuits, yet at the same time hiding her loneliness by plunging herself into the hard work of running a hotel and restaurant.

Beatrice returned and placed the pie in front of Louis. "I baked it this morning," she said proudly.

"*Merci beaucoup, madame,*" he said while reaching for his fork.

Beatrice cupped her hands over her apron and waited for Louis' review.

Louis took a portion of the pie and ate it, slowly chewing and savoring its flavor. With Beatrice locked in suspense, he looked at her and smiled his approval. "*Sensationnel,*" he said.

So, it was on that day that Beatrice and Louis fell in love. For months their courtship became the talk of Chandlers Bend. Some thought that fifteen years too soon for *The Widow Williamson* to throw herself at some foreigner. After all, her husband was a war hero, which demanded respect for his memory. But, as chance, that irresponsible bringer of fate, would have it, they were eventually married.

It was never clear why Louis was on his way to St. Paul in the first place, but no one question it. Deep in the economic depression, many men were seeking jobs, and some had to travel to find work—some paying for passage, while others hopped freight cars and going where destiny took them. So, the assumption remained that Louis Girard happened to be one of many looking for work.

Now, Beatrice Williamson accepted the title of Mrs. Louis Girard with great enthusiasm. When introducing herself to the assortment of travelers that came through her hotel, she would say, with animated articulation, "*Beatrice Girard.*" This pseudo display of association with French aristocracy became a nuisance to her friends and an embarrassment to Louis.

As time went on, Louis was hard-pressed to find some getaway where he could be alone, or at least away from Beatrice. Fortune, once again, that unpredictable harbinger of change, soon smiled on Louis.

It's been said that *some peoples' fortune is others' misfortune.* That change of luck turned out to be true in the case of Tony Amato, the town's barber. Plagued by gout and old age flair-ups, it had become difficult for Tony to stand for long periods.

Now Louis saw salvation in Tony's misery. *"Mon amie,"* Louis began, "ow does one become a barber?"

Tony's scissors paused in mid-cut. "For me, it was easy. My father cut hair as well as his father. So, I guess you could say I was born into it." The scissors began to work their way around Louis' head again. "Why do you ask?"

It was a rare occasion when Louis was the sole customer of Tony's shop, so Louis felt no awkwardness in serving up the truth. "I was wondering, err, if I could learn ze trade?"

Tony smiled. "Yes, but it was years of training and never having cut someone's throat," he said lightheartedly.

"Can *zee* teach me?"

Tony rested his scissors at his side and moved around to face Louis. "Well, I can, and my feet are only too happy to oblige, but I'm not sure anyone in this town would be willing to have you practice on their heads."

"Could you teach me?" Louis asked with wishful pleading.

"Louis, I'll try, but then there is the problem of the license."

"License?" Louis asked, his shoulders and hands rising slightly in puzzlement.

"Let's keep that horse before the cart, Louis. I'll start giving you some lessons after the shop is closed."

*"Merci! Mon amie,"* Louis said and straightened himself in the chair.

As Tony brought his scissors to bear, the shop's doorbell tinkled the arrival of a customer.

"Well, hi, Eddie. How are you doing today?"

"Fine, Mr. Amato. Mom says I needed a haircut. She gimme a quarter. Says I can keep the change." He stood in the doorway, his red hair askew, holding his coin aloft. Eddie was the only son of Albert and Mable Miller. They were the local grocery store owners, called fittingly, Miller's Emporium, for it sold everything from food to lamp oil.

The sun was ducking low behind the west bluff, and with Eddie's entrance, the early spring chill also crept into the shop.

"Close the door, Eddie, and have a seat. I'll tell you what," Tony said, waving a comb in the air, "when I get done with Mr. Girard, you'll be next. And if you can keep a secret, you can have that quarter for yourself."

Eddie smiled, closed the door, and unsuspectingly found a place to sit.

## 2
_____

M able eyed Eddie with some apprehension. "You took a long time in the barbershop," Mable said sternly.

Eddie, a hand set deep into his pocket, played with the solitary quarter. "Mr. Amato said he was going to give me a special haircut, cus I'm special," Eddie said, his voice quaking slightly.

"Humph," Mable uttered. "Well, now that you're here, get in the backroom and sweep up before we leave."

Albert, Mable's husband, locked the front door of their grocery store. "I know that look, Mable. Somethin' bothering you?"

"You could say so. Did you see Eddie's haircut?"

"Yeah. It looks fine to me."

"Maybe to you, it's fine, but I think ol' Tony may be tipping a few while he is working."

"Nah," Albert waved a hand in dismissal. "In all the years I've known him, I've never seen him drink in his shop or even smelled a whiff of booze on him."

"Well, I don't know," Mable said as she collected the cash from the register. "It just looked a little uneven."

Albert took the folding money and placed it in a cloth money bag.

Once Mable turned off all the lights, except one, she joined her husband as he made his way toward the back storage room. " How'd we do today?" Mable asked.

"Four bucks and change, but more on credit," he answered, shaking his head.

"We had a bad winter, but maybe President Roosevelt will get us out of this here depression."

Mable opened the storage door and saw Eddie sweeping up a pile of waste into a dustpan.

She sighed. "I don't know how much longer we can keep running a tab on folks. After all, we got to pay our bills, too."

"Well, FDR's talking bout making changes. We'll see what happens this spring," Albert said as he put the cash into the safe. "Maybe he'll find a way to stop all the misery. People ain't gonna put up with all this sufferin' much longer."

"You know the Suttons owe us nearly five dollars. After their daughter come down with diphtheria, I just don't have the heart to... " Mable trailed off and looked at Eddie with unease. "Eddie, that's good enough," she said as Eddie struggled to push more dirt into the already loaded pan.

Eddie carefully balanced the dustpan and moved toward the trash barrel. With a great show of purpose, he dumped his cargo and tapped the inside of the container to dislodge the last remnants of dust. Triumphantly he returned the pan and retrieved his winter coat. "Are we goin', Momma?"

"Yes, Eddie. We're going," she said in a dull voice. She and Albert pulled off their coats from the wall rack, ready to brace themselves against the cold and damp March night.

Albert and Mable Miller moved to Chandlers Bend when the village was more prosperous, and Eddie was only a baby. It wasn't long before they understood that Eddie wasn't going to be able to ever take care of himself. For a time, Eddie went to the town's school. After several instances of bullying by classmates, the school's principal's professional assessment determined that Eddie was a *disruptive influence*. Albert and Mable agreed he was better off under their tutelage.

With the confluence of trade that the railroads provided, they thought their future was secure and eagerly purchased the local grocery store. The townsfolk called it *Old Man Stanley's* even though it was called Stanley's. To some, Stanley was as old as the surrounding buttes and bluffs. When Stanley Cooper lost his wife to consumption, the sparkle for life that once dwelled in him died, too. That was when he acquired the label of *Old Man Stanley*. After the store changed hands and the new signage erected, Stanley Cooper meekly boarded a southbound train without announcing his destination.

When Chandlers Bend was nearly wiped out, after what residents simply called *The Great Fire*—Albert and Mable's place was spared. Although saved, their business faltered for a time until the townsfolk got back on their feet. Counting their blessing and sympathetic to the community's needs, they became the epicenter for commerce and hope. The following years were eventually profitable, so much so that Albert felt he and his wife should invest in the stock market.

"Mable," he would plead, "everyone is getting rich. We have plenty of money to invest."

As firm as Albert was in spending, so was Mable in saving. "I've been reading," she would say, "that the stock market is running on speculation."

"Well, I read, too," he said defiantly, "I read an article that says women pass on big opportunities that men are taking on credit."

"Mark my word, Albert, you'll be glad we didn't invest."

And so, the battle went on until the crash of 1929. Mable carried with her an aura of superiority following the market's thud. It was sufficient to quash all arguments regarding future spending in the Miller household.

Occasionally, Mable would remind Albert that they would have faced a bleak future if it wasn't for her wisdom. Some covetously viewed the Miller's success not so much with jealousy but anger from those indebted to their generosity. It was one thing to consider another with envy, but irrational resentment tended to fester when that person was obligated to you.

In Chandlers Bend, the "Thou shalt not" of your neighbor's house, wife, and anything else was disregarded by most, but not all, of its citizens. The few that deemed it a holy axiom were either genuinely righteous or a few that were so well off that covetousness was replaced with *false witness against thy neighbor*.

Mable was a beautiful woman. Many of the men in town secretly regarded her with desire. Their wives, although outwardly friendly, felt inferior to her and balanced their inferiority with gossip.

Tall and slim, she wore her blonde hair pulled back into a bun. After Eddie went to bed and her chores done, she would undo her locks. Free of daily demands, she would spend time brushing away the snarls and gaze languidly into her dresser's mirror. Mable, for the most part, was content with her life. Although she loved Albert, sometimes she wondered what her life would have been like, marrying the first man she ever slept with.

Mable's first sexual intimacy was more of an impulse. He was a polished man of the world—she ordinary and naïve. At the time, she envisioned herself following him on exotic voyages—places she only read about in *National Geographic* magazines. He roused her passion for adventure and carnal desire. Defenseless under his spell, she succumbed and surrendered her virginity.

When he abruptly left without word or reason, she was devastated. She hated him as well as herself. Her self-loathing consumed her until she met Albert. She never told Albert of her dalliance because she didn't want to hurt him. He was a kind man. He wasn't the adventurer, but he was loving, as well as a virgin. In her mind, she often thought that if she were to confess her failings, Albert would understand. He would love her just the same. She knew there would be hurt nonetheless. Maybe not so much in the confession, but in keeping the secret from him for so long. This weight of guilt and remorse hung heavily at times.

She slowly brushed her hair.

## 3

To a boy, money in one's pocket burned and needed freedom. There were few places in Chandlers Bend where newfound wealth could be brandished openly. Eddie had enough sense not to spend his quarter at his parent's grocery store. For one thing, most of what he wanted was free for the asking. Besides, even without cost, by asking, Eddie sometimes received a stern refusal. Limited as he was, the only option remaining was Ted's Gas Station on the edge of town.

Ted's, previously a blacksmith's shop, sat on the fringe of the one-time logging road. The road rapidly became a link with Morrisville, the county seat, and adapted to the introduction of the automobile. Ted's father, Jeb Shutter, cursed the day when state work crews arrived and paved the new motorway. His objection was not based on any credible argument. He only hated to see things change. Jeb was a creature of habit and found comfort when things stayed the way they were meant to be. Gradually, he scornfully accepted the progress and grudgingly adapted. By the time there was a steady flow of traffic, his son Ted was old enough to take over.

With Ted in control, Jeb became a fixture on the front porch of the station. From his semi-retirement view, he saw the sputterings of

"Tin Lizzies" and the ghostly silence of the Cadillacs as they came, went, or occasionally raced past.

When a "Duesy" pulled in for a fill, Eddie, excited at the sight, drew closer to its sleek body to gawk, then peeked inside. The owner, a young and attractive woman who wore a plum-colored tailored wool dress, appeared unnerved by the sight of a kid and eyed him with a suspicious glare.

"Get away from the car, Eddie," Ted yelled in a gruff voice.

Eddie retreated but kept staring at the Duesenberg and its female driver.

Ted, standing more erect than usual, sucked in his gut and walked to the driver's side of the car.

The woman rolled down her window and removed her gloves.

"Good morning, ma'am," he sang with a melodic resonance, a tone he only used on out-of-the-area females.

She daintily held out a dollar bill in Ted's direction. "Five gallons," she said haughtily.

When Ted took the money with his grease-ladened hand, she immediately withdrew hers, as if he were a plague carrier.

Ted relaxed his stomach and moved to the rear of the car. He began to fill the top glass cylinder of the pump with gasoline until the desired level. He carefully unscrewed the double-levered handle of the gas cap and slowly inserted the nozzle into the tank with great reverence for the vehicle. Once the gas drained into the car, Ted moved forward to check the oil. Finished, he dutifully cleaned the front window, sneaking at times a quick peek of the comely brunette.

Ted stepped back when he finished, and with a roguish smile, he tipped his hat in a farewell gesture.

The lady countered with a dismissive wave and sped off onto the highway's northbound lane without looking back.

Ted's obnoxious socializing techniques turned most women off. That's not to say that he was without having an occasional fling. The women that found him appealing in one way or another were just as damaged. None of his affairs lasted long. Damaged or not, life with him was not worth the abuse in the long run. If his mother hadn't died when he was only six, perhaps things would have been different. Without a mothers moderating influence, Ted's upbringing and discipline came at the end of a belt.

"What you doing so far away from home, Eddie? You're not running away, are you?" Ted mocked.

"No, Mr. Ted."

Everyone called Ted only by his first name.

"I come to buy a Coka-Cola." Eddie dug into his pocket and revealed his quarter.

"Whadda you do, Eddie, rob a bank? They'll be putting your mug on a poster."

"No, Mr. Ted, I got ... I got ..."

"What's a matter, kid—cat got your tongue?"

Eddie froze.

"I was just joshing you, Eddie. C'mon, I'll get you that Coke."

The soda tub ordinarily contained ice, but March was still in its last vestige of winter, saving Ted the additional expense. Ted pulled out a bottle from the cold water. He snapped off the cap and handed it to Eddie. "That'll be a nickel." Ted held out the Coke with one hand and opened the other for payment.

Eddie dropped the coin into Ted's greasy palm.

"Wow, I don't think I got change for that much money," he said jokingly.

Eddie smiled.

Ted pulled out a fistful of change from his pocket and selected four nickels. "Here you go, kid. Now you got some dough for you and your girlfriend."

Eddie gave him a puzzled look. "I don't have a girlfriend, Mr. Ted."

"Yeah, maybe someday you will, and she'll take all your nickels," he said caustically and then laughed.

Standing there, looking bewildered, Eddie quickly shoved his change back into his pocket.

Ted was about to say something when Olive Perkins pulled up in her Chevrolet Coupé.

Looking matronly with her graying hair pulled into a tight bun, she cautiously stepped out onto the running board before warily placing her laced black Oxfords on the driveway. She never stayed in her car while it was being fueled. She heard that once someone burned to death during the process. In addition to her pyrophobia, she was an inquisitive person who felt that one needed to move about freely to see what was going on.

Ted keep an eye on Olive as she inspected the station like a lioness gazing hungrily upon a herd of zebras. "It's almost on empty, Ted," she said coolly, then caught a glimpse of Eddie. "What's the Miller boy doing here?"

Eddie quickly slipped away behind the gas station's building.

Ted unscrewed the gas cap. "Just getting a Coke, Olive. Not what I'd call a news scoop for your paper."

"Maybe so, but I don't think he should be wandering so far away from home. I have a mind to tell his mother." She changed her focus and looked at the gas pump. "When you going to get a new pump?"

Ted started to pump the gas up into the glass cylinder. "Got one ordered. I should be gettin' it soon."

"Well, now that's a story for the paper."

"Had to get one. With all the traffic, I can hardly keep up. My arm is gettin' tired and ready to fall off."

Olive Perkins made a living being a gossip. Although she was in competition with many of the townsfolk, she had a professional standing with *The Chandlers Bend Telegraph*. She and her husband, Charlie, started their newspaper nine years before the stock market crashed. Like many in town, they continued to eke out a living running small ads and provide the only source for news in the area.

Charlie liked to imbibe now and then, but Olive frowned upon the pastime. A teetotaler by conviction, she was a member of the Temperance League and was angered when the Twenty-first Amendment to the Constitution was ratified. Her condemnations of the use of alcohol and Charlie's failings came into conflict. The only workable solution was for her to be a reporter and general manager, leaving Charlie to run the press and take his medicine as he sought fit. The medicine tag was a holdover from the Prohibition days when he would go to the local pharmacist to have his prescription of brandy filled.

Olive never liked Ted. Like many of the ladies in Chandlers Bend, she found him boorish. That attribute wasn't the sole reason for her dislike of him. When Prohibition became law, he, like many others, exploited the situation by running booze between Saint Paul and Chicago. If Chandlers Bend had another gas station, she would have exclusively patronized it.

"Well, Olive, you're right, fourteen gallons. One more gallon, and you'd be empty." He replaced the gas nozzle on the pump and rubbed his right shoulder. "That'll be two dollars and eighty cents."

She was nearly empty because she intended to use one of the gas stations in the county seat or the town twenty miles north of Chandlers Bend. Her plan didn't work out this time because her business kept her within the immediate area. Approaching empty, she worried that she might get stranded on a backroad, so she relented and filled up at Ted's.

Olive pulled three dollars from her purse. "I need a receipt," she ordered briskly. "Have to keep a record for the paper."

Her request was always the same. Ted cupped the money into his hand and moved to the station. When he came back, he handed her the slip and change without her offering a thank you or goodbye.

Ted turned away and checked to see what had become of Eddie. He caught a glimpse of him nosing around his junkyard. Before he could say anything, another customer rolled into his station.

# 4

The junkyard had an appeal for a kid. Old jalopies became getaway cars or moonshiners dodging a barrage of bullets from lawmen. Eddie sat in the driver's side of a wheelless Model-T, its shell supported by a few terracotta cinder blocks.

The car sputtered to life. "*Ber...room!*" Eddie shouted and grabbed the steering wheel with the passion of a bank robber, making his getaway. "*Ber...room.*" He hunched over to keep from getting shot as his foot barely came in contact with the gas pedal. Eddie looked around and saw the police cars closing in on him. With his index finger, he fired back an endless number of bullets, keeping his pursuers at bay. Eddie yanked on the wheel, causing the car to lean on the turn as he hung on for life. With one hand firmly on the steering wheel, his right hand spun under his left. He fired the last shots before crashing into a make-believe tree, tumbling to the ground and pretending to die.

Eddie got up, brushed himself off, and retrieved his Coke. He gulped the remnants with enthusiasm, letting out a content sigh after.

Ted spotted Eddie heading back to the station. "It's not safe for you to be poking around back there," said Ted. "Your mother is probably wonderin' where you been off to."

He handed the empty bottle back to Ted. "Bye, Mr. Ted," he said and headed back toward town.

Eddie's path home required him to cross the converging tracks of two of the railroad lines. He received numerous words of warning about the dangers of being run over by trains. So, it was with an abundance of caution that he approached.

A trio of kids began moving towards him. They walked between the intersecting east-west rails, and Eddie recognized them from when he went to school. He remembered them as not being very nice, calling him names, and sometimes hitting him when the teacher wasn't looking.

The taller of the group, Bobby O'Dell, called out. "Hey, Eddie, why ain't you at home with your mudder?"

Eddie froze. Despite the chill in the air, Eddie's hands began to perspire. The threesome stopped in front of him. Eddie took a step back.

The two boys flanked Bobby. One wore a felted wool hat, with his wool coat wide open. The other one, capless, was dressed in a heavy knit, frayed sweater. Like Eddie, they all wore brown corduroy pants, but Eddie's were cleaner and not as shabby. Eddie didn't remember their names, only that they were mean to him.

"Yeah, Eddie, why ain't you home?" the kid with the heavy sweater asked.

The one with the cap chimed in. "Go home, Eddie. I hear your mudder calling. 'Come home, Eddie.'"

They all laughed.

Bobby, the tallest of the group, grabbed Eddie by the front of his coat collar. "Got any money, Eddie?"

With a faltering voice, he said, "I ... I got four nickels."

Bobby pulled Eddie closer to him. "Four nickels!" he shouted in his face. "Where did you get all that money?"

"Mr. Ted gave them to me ... told me not to give them to my girlfriend."

"Girlfriend? You got a girlfriend?"

The kid in the sweater yelled. "Eddie's got a girlfriend! Eddie's got a girlfriend!"

"Well, Eddie," the kid with the felt wool cap began as he held out his hand, "I think you should give us those nickels. Hand 'em over."

Eddie shoved both of his hands deep into his pockets and pulled away from Bobby.

The blare of a train's whistle made all the boys turn in its direction.

Bobby rushed Eddie and knocked him down. His partners joined in the assault and pinned his arms to the ground. Eddie squirmed helplessly under their weight. Bobby reached into Eddie's pocket. Finding nothing but a bottle cap, he tried the other one. Four nickels now found a new home in Bobby's greedy hand. The boys eased off, and Eddie struggled to his feet.

Tears streamed freely down Eddie's dirty face. He whined, "Gimme my money."

Two prolonged blasts from the train's horn followed by a short one, then another long one indicated the train was approaching the crossing. A black cloud of smoke trailed from its engine stack. Again, the train blared its approach. The boys dropped back.

It was routine for the east-west train to slow down when traveling through Chandlers Bend cautiously because the tracks crossed the north/south line of another railroad. In passing the group of boys, the engineer and stoker studied them with suspicion. The engineer reached for the whistle's cable and repeated the warning. The boys stepped farther back.

"You want your money, Eddie?" Bobby yelled over the unnerving rattle of the train. "Come and get it." He held up his clenched fist in a dare.

As the train shook the ground beneath them, it made a turn, blocking the engineer's view. The caboose was far behind and would, in due course, round the bend with its conductor and crew.

A series of open-sided wood stock cars slowly moved past them.

Empty of its livestock, the smell still lingered. "Phew!" one of the boys exclaimed.

"It smells like Eddie," Bobby gloated.

A chorus of laughter.

Without a command, the boys began running alongside a solitary flatcar. Eddie followed. One by one, each boy effortlessly pulled himself onto the car.

Bobby O'Dell, his feet dangling over the edge, reached down as Eddie kept pace with the slowly moving car. Bobby held out a closed hand. "Here, Eddie, you can have your money back."

Eddie, anxious and angry, stretched for the cupped hand. Bobby seized Eddie's hand. Eddie's body stiffened. Eddie, no longer walking, twisted and turned helplessly at the edge of the flatcar. The coarse gravel of the train-bed gnawed at Eddie's shoes. His free hand reached for anything he could grasp. The boy in the heavy sweater grabbed it and, together with Bobby, pulled Eddie onto the flatbed.

As quickly as each one of the boys boarded the car, just as quickly, one by one, they jumped from the moving train. None of them landed on their feet. Compensating for the train's momentum, each one dropped, tucked, and rolled onto the grassy berm that bordered the tracks. Mockingly, they waved to Eddie as the train snaked its way away and picked up speed.

Eddie scrambled to his feet, trying precariously to balance himself. The heckling of the trio soon faded. The train began to rush past the flanking treeline. Eddie's brain reeled with indecision. The *thump, thump, thump* from the steel wheels increased in tempo as it passed through a gulch, indicating it was on the straightaway and leaving Chandlers Bend. With wobbly knees, Eddie moved to the edge of the vibrating deck of the flatcar. He stared in horror as the trees became blurs.

In a panic, Eddie jumped.

# 5

Albert and Mable frantically searched every imaginable location that a ten-year-old, full of boyish curiosity, would find tempting. Unable to locate Eddie, they headed to the nearby woods where it was common knowledge that fanciful stories were reenacted by inventive kids within erected boundaries of makeshift forts. Along the way, they asked anyone they met if they had seen him.

Olive Perkins finished locking the front door to the *Chandlers Bend Telegraph* for the night. Before Albert and Mable obtained any information about Eddie, they received guidance on the proper rearing of children—although it wasn't from personal involvement, but through observation.

"Unchecked children become a danger to society," she scolded. "In my experience as a reporter, they turn into hoodlums. I just hope that Eddie doesn't become one of them. The last time I saw him, he was at Ted's gas station, but that was around three this afternoon."

Feeling the stab of anger in the rebuke, Albert and Mable, resentful of her advice, quietly thanked her and made their way toward the edge of town.

In the background, Olive delivered her final chiding. "That's no place for a young boy to be hanging around."

The evening had set in, and Ted's was closed for the night.

As he neared the station, Albert called out, "Eddie! Eddie!" He swept the junkyard with his flashlight's beam. Rats scurried under its probing light.

Mable walked to the house behind the station and knocked on Ted Shutter's door. When Ted answered, he stood in the doorway with his feet set wide in a confrontational stance. Ted's unkempt trousers were supported by a pair of suspenders over a dirty athletic shirt. Mable felt his eyes studying her body.

"The station's closed," he mumbled through a mouth full of food.

After searching the junkyard, Albert came and stood next to his wife and snarled, "Olive Perkins said Eddie was playing around your station earlier today."

Ted swallowed. "Yeah, so what? I told him to get, and he did. Why you askin'?"

"He hasn't come home," replied Mable.

"Hey, if you think—"

"No, Ted." Albert softened his tone. "We're not saying you did anything. We just want to know where he went off to."

Jeb Shutter appeared behind his son. "What's going on? Someone have an accident and needs a towing?"

"No, Pa. The Miller's are looking for Eddie."

"I seen him headin' toward town when I went to use the privy out back," Jeb said, moving closer to the opening. "Yep, it looked like he was talking to the O'Dell boy and a couple of his buddies. I think they was havin' some kinda argument."

Albert and Mable exchanged glances. "Thanks, we need to go," Mable said hurriedly.

While traveling toward the O'Dell place, Albert caught some movement along the east-west railroad tracks, and he aimed his flashlight at the staggering figure.

"Eddie!" Mable shouted and began running blindly in the dark toward her son. She eagerly embraced him, and he emitted a cry of pain.

Albert, close behind, trained his flashlight on his son.

"You're hurt!" She eyed the numerous cuts and bruises on his soiled face.

Albert lifted Eddie into his arms and said, "We got to take Eddie to Doc Brewer's place."

DOCTOR GEORGE BREWER was a veteran of the Great War and experienced combat as a young navy corpsman. After the war, he entered Harvard Medical School, intending to set up practice in some remote Wisconsin village.

*Doc,* as everyone called him, lay on his bed and stared at the ceiling while listening to Bartók's *Piano Concerto Number One* on his record player. His body jerked to attention when he heard wild pounding on his door. In his mid-forties, he was agile enough to spring out of his bed, remove the phonograph's arm, and quickly answer the frantic hammering. As the town's only physician, he was mentally prepared for any crisis, yet he approached each unknown caller with habitual unease.

"Doc, Eddie's been hurt," Mable said as Albert pushed his way through the open doorway.

"Put him over there," Doc Brewer said, pointing to the examination table.

The music over, the swish, swish, swish prompted Doc to quickly lift the phonograph's arm off the record before tending to Eddie.

"What happened to him?"

"We don't know. We found Eddie wandering along the tracks," Mable said while holding one of his hands.

"Eddie, what happened?" Doc asked.

"I fell from a train. I lost all my money."

Examining Eddie's blood-caked head, Doc asked, "You mean, you jumped off a train?"

"Don't know ... maybe."

"Eddie, how much money did you lose?"

"Four nickels for my girlfriend ... I feel funny in my stomach, Mama." Eddie started to cry.

Doc waved a small flashlight past Eddie's eyes.

Eddie recoiled from the beam and wiped away his tears.

Mable gently stroked Eddie's hand. "He doesn't have a girlfriend, Doc. What's wrong with him?"

"Eddie's got 'quite a goose egg' on his noggin. If I can call it that, the good news is he doesn't have any broken bones—just loads of cuts and bruises. Right now, I'm more concerned with what appears to be a concussion. I'll dress his wounds, but we'll have to keep an eye on him."

"Can he go home?" Albert asked.

"Probably not a good idea," Doc said as he went to the icebox. He chipped away a chunk of ice and wrapped it in a towel. He placed it on Eddie's head. "I think he should stay right here. We can take shifts making sure he doesn't fall asleep."

"Why?" Mable asked anxiously.

Doc smiled gently at Albert and Mable while he held the cold compress on Eddie's head, "I don't want to alarm you, but I've seen several soldiers suffer seizures after receiving blows to the head."

"What happened to them?" begged Mable.

Doc did not directly respond, being lost in thought. A member of the Sixth Marines at Belleau Wood, out of the two-hundred there, he was one of only eleven who walked out alive. His mind fought the resurrected images of the shell-shocked, the confused, who aimlessly staggered the battlefield and his futile attempt to save them.

"Listen," he snapped, "things are different now. Eddie will stay right here. We need to keep him immobile and continue to place ice on his head. It will help reduce the swelling." Almost immediately, Doc regretted his unsympathetic tone.

Albert and Mable embraced.

Doc saw their anxiety. "I'll do all I can ... the first few hours are the most critical," he said with more soothing comportment.

---

The first postmaster of Chandlers Bend was Jacob Chandler. After retiring from the logging business, Jacob and his wife Susanna opened a general store. He felt it was easier to outfit loggers, trainmen, and farmers than to do the backbreaking work of chopping wood. Of course, his wife had a lot to say in that decision—this was before the establishment of Miller's Emporium. So, out of demand, he sold such staples as flour, sugar, molasses, nails, cloth, baling wire, and the other necessities for a growing community. With this establishment came the position of postmaster. The advantage of this coincidence meant that Chandler's General Store was guaranteed customers and conversation—or more simply, cash and gossip. This marriage of commerce and communication also made it difficult for any potential rival, which was the case for several years until after *The Great Fire of 1917*.

John Chandler was the only son of Jacob Chandler and the youngest of five. The general rule of a succession of power in Chandlers Bend was based on blood and bullying. Now it was only natural when John Chandler took over the reign of Chandler's General Store that the position of postmaster would be passed on to him.

By the time John took over the store, due to *The Great Fire*, it was smaller than the original. Rebuilt and trimmer in inventory, it faced uphill competition and adaptation to the age of the automobile. Not all of the initial stock was lost in the fire, but it may just as well have been. No longer in demand, the tack gear for a horse collected more dust than interest, as motor vehicles stopped at fueling stations instead of general stores. And that was only part of the problem.

Both John and Mary, to put it delicately, were tattlers. This skill was marvelously honed over the counters of their store. Facts, fictions, and fancy yarns were both born and shared between patron and proprietor. Most of what was said outdid the news from the pages of the *Chandlers Bend Telegraph*.

There can be a problem being the center of information. Sooner or later, your reputation becomes your own undoing, and people acquire an unfavorable opinion of the source. One could argue that sharing important news about your community is a public service, and that is how John and Mary viewed themselves—as public servants.

When the daily mail train came through town, John would wait by the mail crane to exchange outgoing mail for incoming. If improperly handled, letters could fly in all directions in the wake of the passing mail car. John was skilled in the swap, and only once did he encounter any problem, a fault he placed on the train's postal clerk.

That is not to say residents of Chandlers Bend always received their mail in excellent condition. Sometimes, blaming a torn envelope on the improper handling by the trainmen, John waxed on and on about the lack of quality of the newer generation of train postal clerks. In fact, the blame rested more of his outrageous attempts at prying that caused envelopes to become damaged, leaving its contents observable to John's prying eyes. It was said among the townsfolk that if someone died in Chandlers Bend, Death would notify John first.

Breathless, Caroline Dunlop entered Chandler's General Store and was only too eager to unload her news. "Mary, I don't know if you heard, but the Miller boy, Eddie, is near death. He was run over by a train last night."

Shocked, Mary Chandler, busy with straightening cans of paint, turned immediately to hear more. "Who told you?" She drew closer to the counter that divided her from Caroline.

"Ida Moore, Doc Brewer's housekeeper. When she went there this morning, Eddie was lying still on the doctor's examination table. The Doc sent her to the apothecary to get some special medicine. She also said that Albert and Mable were there, too."

"I suppose they're waiting for the end," Mary concluded.

Caroline Dunlop let out a mournful moan and nodded solemnly. "It is indeed a sad thing."

And so, the seed was planted in fertile ground, and like a weed, it sprung, nurtured by mischievous tongues.

---

As Chandlers Bend grew, it was deemed necessary that the rule of law needed to be established. Eli Buchanan was the sixth constable in the succession of lawmen to govern the peace and quiet of its five-hundred or so inhabitants.

Unlike the mayorship, the position of constable was not eagerly sought after. Before accepting the job of lawman as a necessary alternative to starving, Eli and his wife, Barbara, owned a small homestead on the outskirts of town. When Barbara took a fancy to Frank Dawson, the county sheriff, she cleaned out their modest savings account and left town. Humiliated by his wife's infidelity, Eli sank into depression, easing his pain through the neck of a bottle. After losing his home and self-respect, he was easily persuaded to fill the shoes of the departing constable. With the dignity of a new job, he eased off the booze, slightly, and tried to put his life back in order, weathering the malicious gossip of the town.

Amiable to a degree, he looked the other way during the booze-running days of Prohibition, considering it a Federal issue and not his. He showed great sympathy for the enterprising spirit of the bootlegger by purchasing their product—at a discount, of course. His supportive attitude included his own participation as time would allow.

He had a down-home way about himself that proved helpful when defusing a family quarrel or retrieving a lost chicken who suspiciously wandered onto someone else's property. When not imbibing, which was infrequent, he possessed a nattiness for proper attire during special occasions, befitting the office. It was his way of advertising his worth and reclaiming his dignity. Most other times, he felt comfortable in everyday work clothes, making him indistinguishable from the other townsfolk—except when wearing the symbol of his office.

Doc Brewer answered the knock on his door and welcomed Eli.

"You called and asked me to stop by. You have some sort of problem, Doc?" Eli said, paying Albert and Mable Miller a courtesy nod.

Doc caught a whiff of alcohol on Eli's breath.

"Eli, come and have a seat." Doc motioned toward a straight-backed wooden chair. He took the chair on the opposite side of the table.

Eli removed his slouch hat and placed it on the vacant seat next to him. "Has this anything to do with Eddie? I already heard that he was hit by a train."

Eddie, who was propped up against several pillows, stirred but remained quiet.

"I'm not certain about the train hitting him, but I think there's more to the story. I've been up most of the night tending to Eddie, and as near as I can deduce, he jumped off the south-bound three-ten."

Eli glanced at Albert and Mary. "That not at all like Eddie."

"You're right—it doesn't."

"You got a theory, Doc?"

"Near as I can guess, Eddie was pulled onto one of the slow-moving cars and either jumped off on his own or pushed."

Eli stroked his chin. "I have someone in mind, but what's your thought?"

"Bobby O'Dell," Doc shot back.

"I'm not surprised. Other than my personal conviction, why the O'Dell boy? Did Eddie mention his name?"

Doc nodded. "He did, and Jeb Shutter said he saw Bobby picking on Eddie around that time."

"How's he doing?" Eli asked.

"I think the worst is over. I tried to keep Eddie awake most of the evening. I was worried about seizures. I'll tend to him here for a couple more hours before letting him go home. It's been a rough night for everyone."

"Well, Doc, I have to get going." Eli grabbed his hat, then rose from the chair. "I'll stop by the O'Dell place and see what Pete O'Dell has ta say 'bout Bobby."

"Something has to be done about that O'Dell kid," Albert said before Eli was able to reach the door.

"I'll do my best, Al."

It was Saturday, and Pete O'Dell didn't have to work at Clowder's Mill, a gristmill five miles south of Chandlers Bend. Still in bed, he was sleeping off last night's drunk, while his wife Sally was busy hand scrubbing laundry. Bobby O'Dell listened to Tarzan of the Apes, unaware of what was in store for him from the knock on the outside door.

Sally wiped her hands on her apron and went to open the door.

"Sally," Eli began, "is Pete home?"

"Yeah ... he's sleepin'."

Bobby looked up and quickly left the room.

"Can you get him? It's important."

"Come on in, Eli. I'll see if I can wake 'im."

Moments later, a slow-moving Pete, dressed in crumpled trousers and a misshapen athletic shirt, followed Sally into the kitchen.

"What's so important that ya needed to see me so early?" Pete asked hoarsely.

"It's about Bobby."

"Whad'ya mean, 'It's about Bobby?'"

"It appears, somehow, that Bobby pushed Eddie Miller off a moving train."

"He did what?" Pete roared.

"Eddie said—"

"Listen, Eli, that Miller kid ain't' right in the 'ead. That's a fact. So, if you're saying my boy somehow got 'im on a movin' train and then pushed 'im off, I'd say you better look for some other answer."

"Jeb Shutter said he saw your boy arguing with Eddie yesterday."

Pete moved closer to Eli. "That ol' kook. He sits all day watchin' traffic and not much more. Probably a little nuts, too."

Eli cleared his throat. "I'd like to talk to Bobby, myself."

"My boy ain't talkin' to you. I'm not havin' him falsely accused of anythin'. Got that, Eli?"

Eli looked at Sally, who grabbed a nearby chair and appeared to steady herself.

"I can't force you, Pete, but you need to keep a tight reign on Bobby."

Pete brushed past Eli and opened the door. "I'll deal with my boy … now get out."

Eli started for the exit.

When he stepped outside, the door slammed behind him.

Eli knew the kind of punishment Pete would deliver—the same kind of justice his own father administered to him. Eli felt sympathy for Bobby and knew what it was to be abused—the degrading pain and feeling of resentment. He remembered the welts on his backside caused by the sting from his father's belt. He hated his father.

"Bobby!" Pete yelled gruffly. "Get the hell over here!"

The boy appeared petrified, his face ashen. Pete moved quickly around the kitchen table while undoing his thick belt from around his waist.

"Pop, it wasn't me," Bobby pleaded, holding his arms up to thwart the inevitable.

"I don't want anyone comin' to my house and tellin' me how to raise my family. Now get over here!"

He grabbed Bobby by the neck, making him lay face down, splayed over a chair with his bare rear-end exposed for punishment. Bobby, struggling under the forceful hand of his father, began to plead for mercy. Pete drew back the belt and began to whip Bobby's behind. It wasn't until Sally intervened that the beating stopped.

EDDIE, fully recovered, continued to get a free haircut and the sympathy of the town. Likewise, over the ensuing months, the quality of his haircuts also improved. Because of his train experience, he tended to shy away from the railroad tracks most of the time. That's not to say Eddie never went to Ted's gas station. When the urge for a Coke grew in him, and money smoldered in his pocket, begging to be spent, he crossed the tracks with great caution, and only when confident he wouldn't be bothered.

Also, an uneasy truce existed between him and Bobby O'Dell. Like most noteworthy happenings, the event became fodder for gossip, dissected, and studied. Blame was administered, and advice shared among the good people of Chandlers Bend.

When Bobby fell from a train in early autumn and suffered the loss of one of his legs, privately, to a person, except Pete and Sally O'Dell, it was as if the hand of God had the final say. He could be seen hobbling around town on his pegleg, aided by a crutch, but minus his posse. People would look at Bobby and feel sorry for him, yet the nagging belief of divine intervention persisted.

## 8
---

**B**efore any change, there is a lull. Perhaps it is in the weather, and people look skyward. In the distance, they see a wall of clouds that hangs motionless. There is a slight breeze that gently strokes their faces, and they inhale the sweet scent of an approaching shower. Enjoying the freshness in the air, they savor the moment—unaware of what's coming.

Chandlers Bend hung in the balance of change. With only a year into his presidency, FDR's message to reject fear brought new hope to a struggling nation. Unfortunately, that dream was a fantasy and seemingly unattainable for many in Chandlers Bend. Although not suffering as much as the rest of the country, especially Oklahoma, the lack of adequate rain took a toll on their prosperity.

Some did thrive, such as Ted and his transient automobile customers. Beatrice Girard, too, prospered partially from her hotel trade, but it was her culinary abilities that increased her revenue. Her restaurant became a favorite eating spot for a few locals that could afford the luxury of eating out as well as those passing through on the state highway. This also had a trickle-down effect on Louis's midsection. With a year's apprenticeship behind him, he offered to purchase Tony Amato's barbershop. Before he made the offer, Louis had to consult with Beatrice, who held the purse-strings. She immediately consented, seeing it more as a lucrative investment than Louis' retreat.

Louis became a permanent fixture in Tony's barbershop throughout his internship, and no one gave it much thought at the time. What did create a stir was Tony's abrupt departure. Without any fanfare or prior revelation, Tony simply left town.

Customers would enter, look around, and ask, "Where's Tony?"

Louis would merely say, "Monsieur Amato flew ze coop." He would shrug and let out a little laugh as if it were a private joke. In a way, it remained a joke because Louis and Tony were able to keep the transfer of title secret. This wasn't a small matter, considering everything that happened in Chandlers Bend was public knowledge, even before its revelation by the involved participants.

Tony's departure became the subject of speculation for several weeks. A steady stream of customers professed knowledge for his sudden departure based on their recollection of Tony's shared anecdotes. The barbershop became crowded with hearsay.

"He once told me that he wanted to go prospecting in the Dakotas."

Another said, "Tony had a cousin that lived in the Alaska Territory, and he thought it might be fun visiting with him."

"Yah know," someone else said, "I think he had some connections with the Mob—being Italian. Probably someone was gunning for him, and he took a powder. After all, why would he pick up stakes and leave, so sudden like."

"Yeah, I bet that's it."

AND SO, life went on in Chandlers Bend, until that fateful day.

It was not an unusual occurrence to see a stranger in town. After all, Chandlers Bend was intersected by rail and a state highway, so people came and went. But when an unfamiliar face is seen around town and stays, well, that is altogether another matter.

Beatrice looked out her window. The rumble of the four-twenty westbound faded, leaving one female passenger on the platform. The woman, dressed in a charcoal fur-collar Alise Swing Coat, began to walk toward the hotel carrying two suitcases. There was a day when the number of travelers filled the Bluff Side Hotel, which required extra staff. Now, voyagers that needed a room were infrequent. Although there were customers from the state highway, but never like the old days when nearly everyone traveled by rail.

Beatrice held the door open for her.

She was young and attractive—perhaps twenty years old—maybe younger. Beatrice Girard wasn't sure. Her blonde hair, unquestionably dyed, was parted on her left side, and styled with tight finger waves. Her deep-set bedroom eyes suggested trouble, and her shapely figure was ample reason to believe she willingly invited it.

Beatrice instantly disliked her and returned to her position behind the counter.

The girl dropped two bags in front of the hotel's registration desk. The thud of them hitting the floor indicated they were heavy. She made a cursory inspection of the small lobby while shedding her leather gloves. "I'd like a room, please," she said, lackadaisically.

Beatrice probed. "Catching the morning train for Saint Paul?"

"Nope. I'll be staying for at least a week."

Beatrice's hair rose on the back of her neck. "Visiting friends?"

"Nope."

This lack of an explanation agitated Beatrice. She glanced at the suitcases. "A single or double?"

"Single."

"Name?"

"Lucy Lareau."

Beatrice's eyebrows rose slightly. She jotted down the name in the hotel's register. "That'll be five-fifty—in advance."

Lucy removed her purse from her shoulder and rested it on the counter. She pulled out a small wad of bills, stripping off six singles.

Beatrice took note of the size of the bundle and recounted the money. "Dinner is served at six," Beatrice said as she handed Lucy a fifty-cent piece. She took a key off the backboard on the wall and gave it to the young woman. "Your room is down the hall ... number three. The bathrooms are at the end of the hallway. And breakfast is served promptly at seven."

Lucy began to reach for her bags, appeared to hesitate then rested her arms on the counter. "Are there any ballrooms in this burg?" she asked dryly.

Through squinting eyes, Beatrice replied, "Ballrooms?"

"Yeah, like dancing."

"The only dancing around these parts is done on a Saturday night at the village hall."

"What about a saloon? You must have at least one in this burg."

"The Busy Bee is the only tavern in town."

"Is it close by?" Lucy asked impatiently.

Beatrice motioned with her right thumb over her shoulder. "A block down, thataway."

"Thanks." Lucy grabbed her bags and began to move down the hallway.

Curious as to the content of the suitcases, Beatrice called out, "Want a hand?"

Lucy's head turned slightly toward Beatrice. "No, thank you. I'm fine."

Beatrice kept a suspicious eye on Lucy until she disappeared into her room. "That girl is going to be a problem," Beatrice mumbled to herself.

## 9

Gus Severson, along with his wife Stella, were the owners of the Busy Bee. Their business acumen maintained the enterprise through tough times by skillfully sidestepping the law. Originally, it was a saloon that catered to the railroad men, grangers, and dairymen. With Prohibition, the Busy Bee ice cream speakeasy was born. Dressed in the accouterments of its family-friendly façade—the railroad men, grangers, and dairymen continued to drink—only not as openly. The *parlor* atmosphere did bring a certain amount of civility to the previously rowdy clientele. With the repeal of the Eighteenth Amendment to the United States Constitution, it reclaimed its roots.

Gus sat at the far end of the bar and cupped his hand over his left ear, trying to catch the *Kraft Music Hall* radio broadcast over the noise of his customers' squabbling.

"I tells, ya, it ain't right. Puttin' cod liver oil in milk," said Clyde Fisher, a local dairyman. "It just ain't normal."

"Dat's Chicago," Miles Gunter countered. "It won't happen here."

"I tells ya, it—" Clyde fixed his attention to the entrance. Except for the staticky radio broadcast, the room fell silent.

Lucy Lareau strolled into the Busy Bee with purpose. She sized up the place like a fox eyeing the contents of a chicken coop. In addition to her fur-collared coat, Lucy wore a black beret cap, Marlene Dietrich style, that seductively covered a portion of her right eyebrow. She placed a foot firmly on the lower brass rail and rested an arm on the bar's top.

Gus came out of his radio-induced trance and moved toward her. "What'll it be, Miss?" he asked songishly.

"A Gin Rickey."

"Sure thing." He reached for the bottle of gin from the backbar. Throwing a squirt of lime juice in a glass, he followed with the gin and a shot of seltzer.

He slid the drink toward her. "That'll be two-bits, Miss."

She slipped him a buck. "Here, this should hold me for a while." She took a taste. "Not bad," she said after smacking her lips. She took another sip.

Gus laid a hand on the bill. "Catching the morning train to Saint Paul?" he asked before pulling it toward himself.

"No. So, what do people do in this burg for fun?"

He turned toward the cash register and put the dollar alongside it. Gus caught Lucy's reflection, looking at him through the row of bottles in front of the backbar's mirror.

She gave him a wink.

Facing her, he said playfully, "There's the Saturday night dance at the village hall tomorrow. It's gonna be a big event. Some travelin' band from La Crosse is doing the entertainment."

"You asking me out?" she teased.

Turning a shade of red, he stammered, 'No ... no, I was just telling ya ... "

Lucy chuckled, and in mid-laugh, she spotted Eli Buchanan as he ambled in. She turned, supported herself with her elbows, and fixed her back against the bar.

"Hiya, Eli," Gus shouted.

"Things pretty quiet tonight, Gus?"

"Yeah ... normal for a Thursday. Can I get ya something?"

"Taking it easy tonight. Just a Bottle of Schlitz."

Gus knew it was going to be "on the house." During Prohibition, Eli looked the other way when Gus received a new shipment of booze from Saint Paul. Eli also alerted Gus when Federal agents came up from Madison on one of their raids. Gus and Eli laughed about how stupid the agents were. They'd hit a few places in Morrisville before heading north. Well, word spread, and Eli was the first to hear the news. So, as far as Eli was concerned, his drink was paid for.

As Gus turned away to get the beer, Eli gave Lucy the once-over. "Good evening, Miss. Just passing through town?"

Lucy smiled back at him and did an inspection of her own. "Doesn't anyone ever ask, are you new in town?"

Eli let out a loud laugh. "Okay ... are you new in town, Miss—"

"The name's Lucy," she replied and, with her glass, made a salute in his direction. "As far as staying, I've been told the only excitement in this burg is the Saturday night dance."

Gus returned and placed the bottle of beer in front of Eli. He gave the two of them a quick glance and walked back to his perch near the radio.

Eli took a long swig from the bottle. "Well, Morrisville has a movie theater, and that's only about fifteen miles down the road. Of course, ya got to have a car to get there. I know most of the vehicles around these parts. Clyde's Model-T is parked out front along with Miles' Chevrolet pickup. Seeing you're here by yourself, I'm guessing you don't have one."

Lucy undid the buttons on her coat and spread it open. "You're a pretty observant guy," she said flirtatiously.

Eli eyed the plunging neckline on Lucy's navy blue and white lace trim, body-hugging Raileen dress. "Have to be in my job," he said boastfully.

"And what would that be, mister?"

"Name's Eli. I'm the town's constable." He picked up his bottle of beer and took another long pull.

"Wow, a lawman," Lucy said with a coquettish air. "So, Mister, Eli, the lawman, you got a last name?"

"Buchanan."

"You on the job now?"

Eli rested the beer on the bar. He pulled back his three-quarter-length coat to reveal his badge fastened to his blue plaid flannel shirt. "I'm always on the job."

She smiled at his apparent attempt to impress her. "Hey, Eli, my dogs are killing me. Suppose we continue this conversation over there." She pointed to an empty booth on the opposite side of the room. "Unless you got some *copper* stuff to take care of."

He appeared wounded. "No one around these parts ever called me a *copper*."

"Hey, I didn't mean anything by that. It's only a figure of speech. Eli, let me buy you another drink first. Okay? I just thought you had some J. Edgar stuff to do."

He waved it off and, with the same hand, got Gus' attention. "A couple more," Eli said, motioning toward the nearly empty drinks.

Slugging down the remains, Eli picked up his beer and Lucy's cocktail and led the way toward the booth.

When Eli slipped into the booth, Lucy glanced down at his sidearm. "I see you're packing a cannon."

"Yah, a .38 Long Colt," he said and rested his right thumb on gun's hammer.

"Ever use it against any bad guys?" Lucy asked flippantly.

He replied softly, "No." There was an awkward silence. Eli gulped his beer, then cleared his throat. "So, what's your story?"

Lucy played with her glass. "Nothin' much to tell. Born and raised in Milwaukee, moved to Chicago. I got a job as a typist working for a broker at the Chicago Stock Exchange. When it took a tumble, he took a powder out of the tenth floor. Since then, I've worked for any butter-and-egg man who's still in the chips. So, you could say I'm between jobs."

Eli eased back on the bench and studied Lucy. "So, why Chandlers Bend? I would think Chicago's got more opportunity."

Lucy took an unhurried swallow of her drink. "Let's just say that Lake Michigan lost its charm."

"If your planning on finding work here, that'll be next to impossible. Most of the jobs go to the locals. And ya gotta have at least one member of your family buried in the cemetery before you can claim citizenship."

"I'm in no hurry, but I don't think I can afford to stay in the local hotel. Any places around here that take in boarders?"

Eli stroked his chin. "If you're serious about staying, I can ask around for you. Times being what they are, everyone is lookin' for an extra buck."

"I would appreciate that, Eli. After the long train ride, I think I'm going to call it a night." Lucy swallowed the last of her drink.

"It's kinda cold and dark out there. I'd feel better if you'd allow me to give you a ride back to the Bluff Side Hotel."

"I'd like that," she said, moving closer to Eli.

As they began to leave the tavern, Gus called out. "Miss, you have some change coming."

Lucy turned and continued to button her coat. "Suppose that'll keep until my next visit?"

Gus scratched his head. "I guess," he said, looking somewhat puzzled by the statement.

Eli held the door open to his black and tan 1931 Buick Coupé. "The constable business must be pretty good," Lucy said as Eli helped her onto the running board.

"I made some good investments before the crash."

Eli closed the door and went to the other side to start the car. He turned the key, pushed in the clutch all the way, set the choke, pumped the gas, and pushed down hard on the starter peddle. It roared to life.

"Starts pretty good."

Eli reached for the shift and said, "Yeah, it doesn't always. Maybe it's your presence."

Smiling, Lucy turned up her fur collar around her neck. "It's a bit cold in here."

"I'll just adjust the choke a bit, then we'll get going." Eli pointed to the heater set at the bottom of the dash. "It'll take a while to heat up, but I'll get you to your hotel before that happens."

Lucy quietly studied the streets of Chandlers Bend. "Not a lot of activity going on in this burg. Doesn't seem to even need a lawman."

"You'd be surprised. Some of these good citizens are fine until they get a little hooch in 'em."

Lucy laughed. "That's true for any town."

"Well, here we are, the Bluff Side Hotel."

"That was fast, and you're right about the heater," Lucy said with a hint of a shiver in her voice.

Before Eli had a chance to make it to the passenger side of the car, Lucy had already stepped off the running board. "Thanks for the ride," she said and extended a parting hand.

"Was nothin' ... any time." He let loose of Lucy's hand and tapped the brim of his fedora with his right hand. "If ya like, I can take you to the movie theater sometime."

The glow from the hotel's front porch light illuminated her smiling face. "That's a swell idea. Well, goodnight, Eli. Maybe I'll see you at the Saturday night dance?" she said and began to walk away.

"Yeah, maybe," he said while giving her a wave.

"Abyssinia."

Eli laughed then turned away to get back into his car, while Beatrice Girard kept the night watch from her bedroom window.

## 10

W omen never came to the Chandlers Bend's Saturday night dance unattended. By most of the accepted norms of the town, a lady either came with her male escort or in the company of a gaggle of other females friends, but never by herself. So, it was understandable that there was a sudden collective gasp, though muted when Lucy Lareau made her way through the double door entrance of the dance hall. She wore a long, dark-green, sleek sleeveless evening dress—shocking by local standards.

Arranged in a circular fashion around the dance floor were an assortment of tables and chairs, most filled to capacity. There was a specific pecking order to those who occupied the tables. The more prominent the social status, the closer they were to the front stage and sound system. The revelers were neatly dressed—the men in outdated suits and the women in stylish house dresses, adorned with jewelry.

The musical ensemble consisting of a trumpet, trombone, clarinet, bass, piano, and drums played the mesmerizing melody of *Night and Day*. Lucy, with her shoulders back and chest thrust out, sauntered passed the refreshment stand to one of the side tables. Lucy felt the stares of all that were present. "Mind if I join you?" she said to two women occupying a four-chair table at the back.

"No, not at all. My name is Hulda Brown, she said and reached out to shake Lucy's hand. She motioned toward her companion. "And this is my friend Martha McCloskey."

"I'm Lucy Lareau, pleased to make your acquaintance." She placed her purse on the table. Both Hulda and Martha wore Hooverette style housedresses, with robe-like sashes and a front wrap that could be set to either side.

"You must be the new girl in town we heard so much about?" Hulda asked.

"Yeah. I suppose news travels pretty fast in this town," Lucy said.

Both Hulda and Martha let out a nervous laugh.

"I heard you're from Chicago," Martha said with an inquisitive fascination in her tone. "It must have been exciting?"

Lucy smiled. "It's okay, but after a while, the charm wears off—if ya know what I mean."

Again the women laughed in unison.

"You ever see any gangsters?" Martha asked excitedly.

"Not a one. Ya can't believe everything ya read in the newspapers."

Hulda and Martha smiled and exchanged looks.

"What do you gals do in this town for a living?" Lucy asked.

"We're operators for the Lindman Telephone company," said Hulda. "Both of us work the morning shift."

Although young, they were not particularly attractive looking. Hulda, even at her age, looked more matronly while Martha appeared mousy. Lucy thought they could both use a makeover.

"You're lucky to have jobs," Lucy said.

"We know," Hulda answered proudly. "I've been working with the telephone company for five years, and Martha, here, has been working with me for at least three. Right, Martha?"

Martha nodded in a submissive agreement.

"I bet you girls know a lot what goes on around this burg?"

Hulda and Martha traded glances and let out a mutual snicker.

Composing herself, Hulda adjusted her dress and said, "Well, we are sworn to confidentiality."

The truth remained that neither practiced the tenet. Part of the reason for Hulda and Martha's segregation to the rear of the hall was their inclination to gossip. For this reason, many citizens of Chandlers Bend didn't want to add to their rumor inventory. Although Hulda and Martha's job could have been filled by a man, especially during the Depression with so many men out of work, the telephone company felt women were more polite. Another reason for their employment was kinship—both having relatives buried in the local cemetery. That was just the natural order of things in Chandlers Bend.

Lucy, about to say something, stopped and directed her attention toward the entrance. "Who's that?" she asked.

"Oh, my. That's Doc Brewer. He's got a private line," Martha said wistfully.

"He's quite a looker," Lucy said.

Hulda eyed Lucy, then turned toward the foyer. "Everyone in town loves him, and he's nice to talk to. Other than coming to this dance once in a while, he pretty much stays to himself. He does, on occasion, go to Milwaukee and Chicago on business—so we've been told."

Doc caught a glimpse of Lucy, but it was Hulda's wave that drew him toward their table.

The collection of revelers trained their eyes on Doc, but it was shortlived when the song *My Extraordinary Gal* started to be played, and a flood of people swarmed onto the dance floor.

"Good evening, Hulda," Doc said over the loud music, then nodded to Martha, "You're both looking fine this evening. Mind if I join you?"

Hulda motioned toward the empty chair. "Sure thing, Doc. Have a seat." She waved her hand. "Doc, this is Lucy Lareau, she's new in town."

Before sitting, he extended a hand, which Lucy took. "My given name is George Brewer, but as you just heard, most people just call me Doc."

"Pleased to meet you ... Doc, I'm sure," Lucy said.

Gradually releasing her hand, he sat down.

"Well, I'm feeling pretty good tonight. I just came from the Thompson place and helped deliver a healthy little girl. It was a tough delivery, but everything turned out fine. I feel like dancing," he said. "Hulda, wanna cut up the rug?"

Hulda looked a little surprised and enthusiastically got up. "Lead the way, Doc."

Martha and Lucy watched for a while as the dancers gyrated on the dance floor, with Dr. Brewer and Hulda blending into the group.

Lucy turned toward Martha. "It doesn't look like they serve anything but punch here. Any chance of getting anything stiffer?"

Martha reached down and hauled up a paper bag and partially pulled out the neck of a bottle. "They don't serve liquor here. Ya gotta bring your own. Go get yourself a glass of punch, and I'll spike it for you."

When Lucy returned, Martha, topped off her drink just as Dr. Brewer and Hulda came back to the table.

"Wow, that sure got the blood circulating," Dr. Brewer said.

Before putting the bottle down, Martha displayed it to Dr. Brewer. "Care for some, Doc?"

He waved a hand in her direction. "Nah, gotta keep sober in this job. When I catch my breath, I'll take you for a spin. How's that sound.'

"Anytime you're ready, Doc," Martha said.

When *Let's do the Breakaway* started, accompanied by a male vocalist and fueled by under-the-table booze, the Saturday night shindig roared into full swing. *The Charleston* followed, challenging the Roaring Twenties generation into thinking they could still do it, and the young feeling emboldened to give it a try.

Martha started to drag Dr. Brewer off his chair. "You promised," she implored.

"I'm too old for that," he protested. "I did that when I was a kid."

Martha won out. After the dance, Dr. Brewer returned puffing. "No more fast ones for me," he said wheezing.

Following some polite table conversation about the weather and the economy, *Moon Glow* slowed down the pace. Lucy looked at Dr. Brewer and said seductively, "Now it's my turn."

Dr. Brewer nodded willingly. "A slow one I can handle."

Under the dim lights and soft music, Lucy pushed her body close to Doc's. She felt his interest. She smiled temptingly and rested her head on his shoulder. When the music stopped, they still held their embrace for a while longer before returning to the table.

The entertainment ended with Duke Ellington's *Sophisticated Lady,* with Dr. Brewer and Lucy swaying to the final dance.

Hulda and Martha didn't have the room in their 1929 Model A Ford for another passenger, so Dr. Brewer offered Lucy a ride back to her hotel.

BEATRICE GIRARD, alerted by the slamming of a car door, slipped out of bed and took up her post at the bedroom window.

"I had a wonderful time," Lucy said. "Thanks for the ride, Doc."

Dr. Brewer put his left hand on the door handle, ready to open it. "I don't go very often to the town dances. I had some concern for Lilly Thomson and her baby, but everything turned out okay. That put me in a good mood and just wanted to be around people tonight."

"I'm glad you did."

"If you're still going to be in town, I could take you there next week."

"On a date?" Lucy asked.

"I guess you could call it that."

"I don't know. I'm trying to find a job, and I can't afford to stay too long in this hotel."

"I know a lot of people in this town, and some of them owe me a favor or two. I'll see what I can do."

"That'll be swell. Don't bother to get out and help me. I can manage." Lucy leaned over and gave Dr. Brewer a light kiss on the cheek. "You're sweet," she said, then opened her own car door and stepped out. She gave him a wave as the car gradually pulled away.

With nothing more to hold her interest, Beatrice, too, moved away from her post and went back to bed.

## 11

F udge was not his real name. His real name was Vincent James Spencer. Most everyone called him Fudge because, as a young kid, he loved to eat chocolate bars at the movie theater and not very tidy in doing so. When he got older, his eating habits improved, but like the gooey residue of a candy bar, the label stuck.

Vincent's true identity, preserved through the educational system, had little tolerance for nicknames. His mother, a stickler for perfection, and his employer, *The Chandlers Bend Telegraph*, as a matter of habit, also shunned the practice.

"There's your papers, Vincent," Olive Perkins said, pointing. She presented him with a sheet of paper where he dutifully signed his name, guaranteeing that he would repay the newspaper $3.78 for the week. With 75 customers, Vincent cleared $3.72 for himself—that is, if every customer paid him the ten cents per week subscription rate. That's not always an easy task when every penny counted, and most everyone had a hard-luck story at collection time.

When The Great War began and his father, Jim, was drafted, his mother, Helen, feared for his father Jim's life. The fear became a reality and so devastating for his mother that she came close to losing

Vincent through sheer grief. Adding to that sorrow, both of Vincent's grandparents died from the Spanish Flu. After his mother settled all accounts, it left her with an inheritance that barely sustained them. This was Vincent's world, and he cheerfully accepted its reality.

Fortunately for Vincent's mother, when the stock market crashed, the mortgage on her parent's home was already paid. Determined to keep what little she had, Helen took in boarders and ran a laundry business out of her house. In her mid-thirties, still, a beautiful woman, the economic and emotional strain added unforgiving years to her striking but stern features.

Vincent's mother had a few suitors. He saw them as being abusive or downright lazy. Some were intolerant of Vincent. When he graduated from eighth-grade, he assumed more responsibility, and at the age of thirteen, began to work for the newspaper. Although Vincent gave his mother money, she insisted that he save some of it for his own future and education.

After reading the front-page headlines and skimming the rest of the news, Vincent hurriedly folded the evening edition of the paper into a tight roll. He stuffed them into his canvas bag and began walking his route. Tall, lean, and muscular, he was viewed by many local girls as quite the catch. Many of them would wait for his arrival and eagerly retrieve their parent's newspapers from him using the excuse of assisting Vincent.

Caroline Dunlop was older, and not an impressionable young girl. Without a hobby, boyfriend, or useful profession, her interest was simply one of nosiness. Her passion for gossip was tolerated by her elderly, doting parents who feared being left alone.

Caroline walked out of her front door and met Vincent half-way. "Hi, Fudge, what's new today?" she said in her usual inquisitive fashion.

To which, Fudge would typically say, "Nothing much."

But today was different.

"A whole bunch of stuff," he said, his voice rising with excitement. Without a "hiya" or "good evening," he excitedly continued. "The Dillinger Gang is hiding out somewhere in upper Michigan. The police found their hideaway in Saint Paul, and there was a gun battle. They're sayin' Dillinger's been wounded, and—"

"Fudge, stop your jabbering and give me the paper," she said and held out her hand. Without so much as a thank you, she whirled around, unfolded the paper, and quickly returned to her cottage, browsing the headlines as she went.

Fudge never had the exciting experience of standing on a street corner and yelling, "Extree! Extree! Read all about it," as he had seen the movies. Now, with the news of Dillinger on the loose, he wanted to shout it about town as he swiftly went from house to house. Most of the time, he flung the paper on a doorstep or walkway, except when it rained and wasn't able to share the excitement of the day's news.

When Vincent did encounter someone, his enthusiasm gushed out of him like steam from a pressure cooker, and he blabbered, "Dillinger and his gang are on the loose." Only the young girls would listen. The adults, like Caroline Dunlop, would snatch the paper from him and eagerly read the details for themselves.

The excitement of bank robbers rekindled Vincent's dream of becoming a newspaper reporter, a fantasy privately nurtured and kept from his mother until only recently. Times were tough, and a journalist's education wasn't in the cards for him. Yet he fantasized about someday breaking the big scoop.

"Hey, Fudge, what's got you so lathered up?" Eli Buchanan asked.

"The Dillinger Gang is on the loose."

"Not around these parts, Fudge. They're a ways away. I'm pretty sure we don't have anything to worry about here in Chandlers Bend. But, I'll be keeping an eye out for them, just in case."

With uneasiness set deep into his eyes, Vincent said, "He's all over the place—Racine, Chicago, Sioux Falls. He's everywhere, Mr. Buchanan."

"Don't waste your time thinking about him. I heard over two hundred lawmen are tracking him down. It's a matter of time."

"Well, I don't know. The police haven't caught Dillinger yet."

"Trust me, they will," Eli said and began to walk away. He stopped and turned back to Vincent. "Fudge, is your mom looking for boarders?"

Vincent gave Eli a puzzled look. "She was renting out the room across from mine on the second floor—a Mr. Evers. He works at the grist mill."

"You said she *was*. So, it's vacant now?"

"Yes, sir. You ain't thinking of looking for another place, are you?"

Eli shook his head. "No, not at all. Hey, I shouldn't be troubling you, I'm keeping you from your job. Run along, Fudge. I'll stop by your mom and have a talk with her."

Eli knew Helen when she was Helen Marquart. He liked her and, at times, held her in high regard, but there were the social conventionalities that kept them apart. The fact she was one year behind him in grade school prevented their socializing.

When Eli joined the army, Helen became engaged. Later, when her husband died, he had already married Barbara Mason. After Barbara left him, Eli soured on the thought of getting married again and took to drinking to compensate for the loss.

When Helen Spencer came to the door, she appeared uneasy. Crossing her hands to her breast, she asked, "Nothing wrong, is there, Eli?"

He gave her a reassuring smile. "No, not at all, Helen. Mind if I come in?"

"Sure, come on in." Helen drew back and opened the door. "Have a seat." She motioned toward the kitchen table.

Eli gave the kitchen a brief once-over. He saw a large pot simmering on the stove, and the air had the unmistakable aroma of potatoes cooking. There were also the obvious clues of hardship that pervaded most residences during the Depression. Helen Spencer's home was no exception from the faded drapes to the neat pile of dried corncobs next to the kitchen stove.

Helen caught Eli eyeing the cobs. "Sam Doggers used to bring those home from the mill. That's the last of the load. It helps save on the firewood."

"I was just talking with Fudge before coming here."

She gave him a quick look. "You said nothing's wrong. He's not in any kind of trouble, is he?"

Eli shook his head and laughed. "No, no, nothing like that. You raised a good kid. He told me that you may have a spare room to rent."

Still standing, she asked, "For you?"

"No, for a friend?"

Helen took a seat on the other side of the table. "Yeah. That was Sam's room. When they cut his wages, he wanted me to give him a break and charge him less money. I couldn't afford to lower the rent. He didn't tell me where he was going. With less money coming in, I figured it's better to have an empty room than have another mouth to feed.

"This friend of yours, someone I know?"

"Well, she's not really—"

"She?"

Eli blushed slightly. "It's not what you think. I just met her, and she appears to be down on her luck."

"I'm not running some sort of charity, Eli," Helen snapped. "I'm assuming she's got some money?"

"Well, I'm sure she does. She ain't destitute or anything like that ... only ... ah ... she's between jobs. She's a classy dresser."

"Humph," Hellen said under her breath. "Since when did you become a fashion reviewer? Tell your *friend* it's twelve dollars a month, including a small breakfast and dinner ... laundry's extra. Where is she staying now?"

"She's got a room at the Bluff Side Hotel.

"I'll stop by and talk with Beatrice and see what she has to say. In the meantime, you can let her know ahead of time ... no smoking or cooking in the room. I don't want anyone to burn down this place. I really don't like taking in total strangers, but I can certainly use the money."

Eli began to rise. "Thanks, Helen. I'm sure you won't regret it."

## 12

E velyn Ferris looked up from her teller's cage window. "Eli! You gave me quite a start, coming in here holding that shot- gun. You expecting trouble?"

Eli, cradling his pump-action gun in his right hand, gave it a pat with his left and smiled. "With the Dillinger Gang on the loose, I'm not taking any chances."

Bill Larsen, the bank manager, came out from the back room. "Hi, Eli. Glad to see you." He eyed Eli's gun. "You plan on hanging around in the bank until Dillinger is caught?"

"Well, I sorta thought I'd hang around outside in my car and keep an eye on the place for a few days—at least until I get a better idea of where Dillinger is. I just stopped in to tell you of my plans and to let you know that I hired Henry Blake as my deputy until this business blows over."

"Where's Henry, now?" Larsen asked gruffly.

Eli pointed to the building across the street. "I have him sitting in that second-floor apartment during bank hours. He owns a Spring- field .30-06, and he's a damn good shot."

"This Dillinger stuff got everyone on edge. First, I heard that there was a shootout in Saint Paul, now I just heard he robbed a police arsenal in Warsaw, Indiana. They got more guns and some bullet-proof vests. He appears to be everywhere."

"Yeah, I know, Bill. One good thing is he hasn't been seen around these parts."

"So far," Bill Larsen countered.

"I'll be around if that happens," Eli said tersely before turning away. Within a few dozen steps, he was outside.

As he approached his Buick Coupé, Lucy Lareau greeted him with a warm smile.

She glanced at his shotgun. "Wow, bringing out the big guns, are ya."

He came to a halt and cradled his gun over his chest. "People are all worked up about the possibility that the Dillinger Gang may show up in town. Personally, I don't think we have to worry, but it gives folks some peace of mind." Eli detected an uneasiness that spread across her face and asked, "You all right?"

"Yea, sure. Just don't like the idea of bank robbers shooting up the town," she said, then perked up a bit. "Hey, I'd like to thank you for fixin' me up with a room. Helen Spencer said you'd put in a good word for me."

"Yep, it's the least I could do for an old friend."

She laughed. "Yeah, sure. We've been friends for … I'd say at least two days."

"At least," he said with a smile.

"Hey, Eli, speaking of our friendship, why didn't you come to the village hall last week Saturday?"

"I had every intention of going to it, but a police matter came up."

"Police matter? Big ol' bad gangsters?"

He laughed dismissively. "No, nothing like that. There was a serious accident on the state highway. Some guy and his wife were traveling home in his old flivver, and it ran off the road. He smashed into a tree, killing both of them."

"Was drinking involved?"

"There wasn't any sign of that being the cause. My guess, the guy, swerved off the road to avoid hitting a deer. Happens all the time in these parts. Not necessarily killings the occupants of the car."

"Oh, I'm sorry to hear that. Were those folks from around here?"

"No. Their identification said they were from a town in Iowa."

"It must be hard to deal with," Lucy began. "I mean, all the blood and torn bodies?"

"I try not to think about it too much," Eli said indifferently. "It's part of the job."

Lucy's searching look made Eli feel uneasy.

Eli cleared his throat. "Seeing I missed the dance, I'd like to make it up to you and take you to a picture show. There's a new Tarzan movie playing in the county seat."

"I'd really like that, Eli, but I just got a job, and I have to check with Doc before I make any plans."

"You got a job working for Doc?" he asked, taken aback by the news.

"Yeah. Doc told me his files are a mess and asked if I'd be interested in working for him."

Eli adjusted his hold on the shotgun and stepped back. "It appears your going to do all right for yourself. And speaking of doing, I best be moving on and taking care of business myself. I'll stop by Helen's house and see when you're free." His left hand took control of the gun, and he tipped his hat slightly in a goodbye salute.

"Abyssinia," she said in parting.

Eli sulked his way back to his car. He opened the passenger side door and carefully set the gun in place before moving to the driver's side. Once inside, he fetched a pint of whiskey from under the front seat, removed the cap, and discreetly took a long gulp.

## 13

L ouis Girard closed the shades to block the late April's sun from overheating his barbershop when the door shot open. "The FBI cornered the Dillinger Gang," Fudge yelled as he wielded a lone newspaper in the air like a club. His canvas newspaper bag hung limply off his shoulder.

"Maître Fudge, relax ou you'll die of ze heart attack," Girard said before snatching the paper from Fudge's waving hand.

Vincent Spencer turned around with as much eagerness in entering, bolted back into the street, and made his way home.

"Mom!" he called out, "The FBI had a shootout with the Dillinger Gang near Rhinelander."

"You can tell me all about it during supper. Now wash that newspaper ink off your hands before we sit down to eat."

Lucy Lareau almost collided with Vincent as he charged up the stairs. "Whoa, Vincent," she said. "What's all the commotion about?"

He paused, mid-flight. "The Dillinger Gang was up-north, and there was a shootout with the FBI," he stammered before briskly continuing his upward flight.

When Lucy entered the kitchen, she asked, "Helen, may I see tonight's newspaper?"

Helen handed the paper to her. "I set it aside until after we had our dinner."

"Thanks, I only want to see what Vincent is so excited about."

"Oh, that boy, he loves his job and gets pretty excited when there's a big story on the front page."

Clutching the paper, Lucy left the kitchen.

When dinner was called, and everyone had assembled around the table, Vincent impatiently rehashed the news. Helen sensed a change in Lucy's demeanor. "Something troubling you, Miss Lareau?"

Appearing unenergetic, she said, "It's too bad we are in this financial mess. With all the crime and killings…" She trailed off.

"I agree," Helen said softly.

The table conversation ceased, and even Vincent's enthusiasm retreated under the heaviness of the solemn mood. Only the clinking noise of utensils striking the plates remained until Lucy spoke up. "Helen, would you like to join me for a drink or two at the Busy Bee tonight?"

Vincent shot a probing glance at his mom.

"I don't know. I have to clean up and do the dishes."

"Helen, when was the last time you went out? I'll tell you what, Vincent, and I will help you clean up.

"Sure, Mom. I'll help," said Vincent willingly.

Lucy smiled. "And the drinks are on me tonight. How about it?"

Helen's face signaled her fascination at the prospect. "Okay, but not too long. I do have a lot of work to do tomorrow."

THE BUSY BEE BAR, or The Triple B, as some of the locals called it, was empty of customers. Gus Severson, along with his wife Stella, sat at the far end of the bar. Father Coughlin's nightly radio broadcast was holding their interest.

Gus looked up and hurried down to the end of the bar. "What can I get for you, ladies?" He studied Helen before switching his attention back to Lucy.

"A Gin Rickey for me," answered Lucy. "And I think I got some credit coming from my last visit."

Gus looked puzzled. "Ah... I don't—"

"Hey, I'm just funning ya, Gus," Lucy said, slapping a dollar bill on the bar. She looked at Helen. "Your turn."

"Hmm ... just a glass of wine, please," Helen said timidly.

"Why don't you ladies have a seat, and I'll bring your drinks out to you." Once more, he examined Helen with interest.

Lucy led the way to the spot that she had previously occupied on her first visit.

Both Helen and Lucy removed their coats. They hung them on the hooks fastened to the posts on either side of the partition separating the adjoining booths.

"Thanks for coming with me," Lucy began. "I didn't feel like staying in my room alone tonight. I just wanted to get out."

"No. Thank you. This is really a treat for me. Did you spot how Gus reacted to me being here?"

Lucy nodded.

"I've often thought of coming here by myself, but... you know, I don't want to—"

"Give the town something to talk about."

"You got that right."

Both of them laughed in unison.

"Listen, sister, where I come from, you don't have to worry about some old biddy shooting off her mouth at the church social," Lucy said with contempt. "Now tell me the truth, what did Beatrice have to say about me?"

Helen shifted in place and cleared her throat. "She didn't say too much, except... ah... she thought you were a Sheba."

Lucy let out a sonorous laugh. "That's exactly what I mean by some old biddy."

Gus came to the table, holding a tray with their drinks, while his wife Stella divided her attention between her husband's task and Father Coughlin. "Here ya go, ladies," he said, placing the drinks in front of them. He dropped a fifty-cent piece on the table.

Lucy grabbed the coin and put it back onto Gus' tray. "That's for the next round."

When Gus was out of earshot, Lucy leaned forward. "I'll bet she's said something about you too, sister. I know the type. I can spot them a mile away."

"Miss Lareau, a word of advice, and I mean it in the nicest way, some of the townsfolk have little to do except talk." She glanced up and saw Stella keeping an eye on them. In a softer voice, she continued. "So, I guess what I'm saying is be careful what you say in public."

"First of all, you can skip the Miss part. Just call me Lucy. Okay?"

"Sure thing ... Lucy, but at the house, I'd just as soon call you Miss Lareau. You see, I've been trying to raise my boy properly—you know, being courteous and polite."

"Gotcha," Lucy replied smartly, picked up her drink and toasted. "Here's to old bats and noisy spinsters."

Helen smiled and responded with a wave of her wine glass and took a sip of her drink. She rested her glass. "Lucy, you are a most unusual woman."

"I'm going to take that as a compliment."

"It was," Helen said earnestly. "Now tell me the truth. Chandlers Bend isn't exactly the kind of town a big city girl like you belongs in. My thoughts are my own, and I haven't shared them with anyone, even Vincent. I figured you're either running away from something or running to somebody. Which is it?"

Lucy eased back slightly and appeared to give the question some thought. Finally, she said, "It's the latter—and it's a man."

Helen nodded. "Isn't it always?"

"He was supposed to meet me here a couple of weeks ago, within a day or two of my arrival in this burg. I don't know exactly where he is, but he knows where I am."

Helen looked attentively at Lucy. "He's married, isn't he?"

Lucy vigorously shook her head. "No, not exactly. I think he's got another girlfriend, but I can't be sure."

"So, you plan on sticking around town until he shows up?"

"Uh-huh," Lucy said with a snivel.

"How long do you think that will be?"

The toughness in Lucy appeared to melt. "I don't know. Right now, I don't have any other plans. As I said, he knows where I am."

"This man got a name?"

"Jack."

"Jack?"

"Yeah, Jack."

After a lengthy silence, Lucy said, "Enough about me. Drink up, and let's have one more." She downed her Gin Rickey before waving the empty glass toward Gus. "A couple more of the same."

Lucy turned back to Helen. "And what about you, Helen, what's your story? In my opinion, you don't belong in this town any more than I do."

"I hate this town," Helen said with controlled resentment. "I've wanted to say that out loud for years. If I were to admit that to anyone in this town, I'd be shunned, and I don't know what would happen to Vincent or me."

"Why are you telling me this?" asked Lucy.

"Because I just needed someone to hear me say that. I figure, sooner or later, you're gonna leave Chandlers Bend and take my secret with you."

As Gus approached their table, Helen and Lucy paused their discussion.

"Thanks, Gus," Helen said uneasily.

Gus dropped off the order and recovered the spent glasses. He gave the two of them a questioning look but said nothing and promptly left.

"What's his story?" Lucy asked.

"Before Prohibition, this place was a saloon. Once the town went dry, he and his wife converted it into an ice cream parlor." Helen laughed as if she just told a joke. "There was probably more booze drunk in this place than ice cream during those dry years. Now he's a pillar of the community. It just goes to show you. The corrupt get more corrupt and powerful."

"You sound bitter."

"Sure, I am. I work six days a week, scrimping and saving, just to make ends meet, and that bastard wallows in ill-gotten money. Between you and me, I'm kinda rootin' for those who rob banks.

Lucy said nothing, smiled broadly and reached for her drink.

## 14

D r. George Brewer answered the hesitant knock on his door. Opening it, he was greeted by the smiling face of Lucy Lareau.

"Good Morning, Doc, reporting for duty," she said enthusiastically.

George Brewer felt embarrassed standing in his stocking feet, his suspenders loosely hanging to his sides, and wearing only an athletic undershirt. "Sorry for my appearance. I wasn't expecting you so early."

"Ya, you know what they say about the early-bird, don't ya, Doc?"

"Yes, I do, but I'm not serving worms today."

Lucy snickered and began to take off her coat. "Ya got a place for this?"

George Brewer reached out. "Here, give that to me. I'll hang it on this rack by the wall."

Lucy Lareau slowly moved into the center of the room.

"I better get dressed. My housekeeper Ida will be here shortly, and I don't want her to get the wrong impression," George Brewer said and began to walk toward his bedroom door, which was ajar.

"The people in this town sure like to talk, don't they?" Lucy commented as the smile grew across her face.

"Yes, they do," he said stoically and disappeared into his bedroom.

No sooner was Dr. Brewer gone before the outside entrance door opened. A thin, older woman with graying hair, wire-framed glasses, and a guarded look walked in and eyed Lucy with interest. "Does Doc Brewer know you're here?" she asked with an accusatory glare.

"Yeah, I'm his new assistant, Lucy Lareau. And you must be Ida."

Ida appeared bemused. She stared at Lucy with hard eyes. "Are you a nurse?" she asked with an air of disapproval.

Lucy moved about the room in total indifference while looking at the wall decorations and medical honors.

*You can quit the dumb act, lady; you have already have made up your mind about me from the other gossips in this burg.*

"I'm more of a secretary," Lucy said glibly.

"And what does that involve?" Ida asked coldly.

A spiteful grin formed on Lucy's face. "I put order anywhere there's a mess."

Just then, Dr. Brewer returned from his bedroom. He now wore a white dress shirt, a green striped necktie, and his suspenders were firmly in place on his shoulders. "Hi, Ida. I assume you met my new secretary?"

"Yes, Doc. We had a nice little chat, we did." Ida, leaving a chill behind, moved toward the utility closet.

"Good. Lucy, why don't you come with me, and I'll show you where I keep my records," Doc Brewer said and motioned to Lucy for her to follow him. He led her into a back room and reached for a pull chain that dangled from a bare-bulb ceiling light fixture. Against the wall, a large oak, rolltop desk stood, flanked by two wood filing cabinets.

"It's a bit crowded in here," Lucy said.

"For what I have to do, it's fine." He fumbled for the light pull on a green-shaded desk lamp. "This should give you enough light."

Lucy scrutinized the small stack of papers and file folders resting on the desk. "It doesn't look like it will take me too long to organize that." She pointed at the pile.

He laughed. "Well, have a look inside these cabinets," Dr. Brewer said and jerked open a couple of drawers. A few papers fluttered down to the floor from the overstuffed interior. "You can see that I'm not very organized, but I manage to find what I need. Although, lately, I've been having to spend more time searching than I care to." He asked, jokingly, "Well, Lucy, you up to the task?"

"I'll give it my best shot, and on the plus side, it would appear there's job security in this doctoring stuff."

Dr. Brewer laughed. "Well, you got grit, and that goes a long way in *doctoring stuff*. My patients will be coming in soon. So, I'll let you be."

"Got ya, Doc. See you later," she said and turned toward the desk.

FOUR PATIENTS WERE ALREADY SITTING in the waiting room when Doc entered. He eyed Bobby O'Dell with his mother. "Hi, Sally," he greeted. "And how you doing, Bobby?"

"My legs botherin' me," he said without emotion.

"I've been rubbing it with that salve you gave me, Doc," Sally said defensively.

"Come on, Bobby, let's have a look at that leg in my office."

When they entered Doc's office, Bobby immediately scooted onto the examination table. He pulled up the trouser that covered his pegleg.

"Not so fast, Bobby. Why don't you come on down and stand on the floor first," Doc Brewer said calmly.

Bobby jumped down.

"Now walk toward the door, Bobby and then come back and sit on the table again."

Doc Brewer observed Bobby's movements and looked at Sally,

who was wringing her hands in apparent stress. "Don't look so worried, Sally," Doc Brewer said gently. "Bobby is growing, and he only needs a new prosthesis."

"Doc, we ain't got money for a new pro... whatever you call it."

"Don't worry about that, Sally. Ed Sanders owes me a favor. I'll take some measurements off Bobby's leg and run them down to the sawmill in Hadley later on today. I'll have him fix Bobby up with a new oak leg. I don't know exactly how long it will take, Ed, but in the meantime, Bobby, try not to overdo it. The size difference between your pegleg and other leg is throwing your gait off."

Sally rose and reached out to grab both of Doc Brewer's hands. "Thank you, thank you very much, Doc. I was worried, sick."

"Think nothing of it, Sally. I'm glad that I was able to help." Doc looked at Bobby. "And you, young man, I have something for you."

Doc Brewer went to his bookcase. He reached for a book and handed it to Bobby. "Here, Bobby, give your leg a rest and read this."

Bobby accepted it and read out loud the title. "*Treasure Island.*"

"Yes, Bobby, you'll love it. It's a tale about the high seas—pirates and buried treasure. When you get done with it, I'm guessing your new leg will be ready. When you come back, we'll talk about the story. How does that sound, Bobby?"

Bobby looked at him dubiously. "I guess so."

"Well, give it a try," Doc said and ushered them out to get his next patient.

Dr. Brewer's phone began to ring as he went back into his office for his next case. When he put the receiver to his ear, he heard a panicky voice call for help at the same time the outside door sprang open.

"Doc!" Eli Buchanan shouted while steadying himself between the doorknob and doorframe. "You gotta come quick. There's been an accident on the main road, on the edge of town. Come on—I'll give you a ride."

"Eli's here!" Doc exclaimed into the phone. "We're on our way." He slammed down the receiver and hurriedly grabbed his black medical bag, pausing only briefly to snatch his jacket off the wall hook.

"How bad is it?" Doc asked Eli as they sped away.

"It's bad. I think one person is dead, and two others seriously injured." Eli began to pound on the horn, forcing a few pedestrians to scatter. "When I got there, several people were already on scene and giving aid. I figured the best thing I could do was get you."

"Any idea of how it happened?"

Eli shook his head wildly. "It just looks like someone went through the intersection without stopping. The car going east was broadsided by the one going north."

Their car sped across the train tracks and rounded the bend. As they neared the intersection, Ted's gas station came into view. It was clogged with vehicles and the curious. Eli pounded angrily on the car's horn. People not involved in helping the injured began to move back.

Eli's car was still moving as Dr. Brewer swung open his door and stood on the running board. Firmly gripping the door, his other hand clung to his medical bag that rested on the seat. When the car came to a stop, Doc jumped off and rushed to the side of the closest victim.

The twisted remains no longer resembled any identifiable manu-facturer, except the disconnected wheels indicated that they were once automobiles. The immobile body of a man, his head strangely twisted, lay curled on the roadway. From his mouth, a pool of blood turned the road crimson.

"Get outta my way!" Dr. Brewer yelled. Two men, who stood between him and the man, moved back. Doc dropped to the pave-ment. He snatched his stethoscope from his valise, and hurriedly checked for a heartbeat. He found none. Rising from his kneeling position, he promptly went to the victims of the other car. The driver appeared pale, his skin cold to the touch, and blood seeped from the man's nose. Doc looked up and saw a woman on the car's passenger side, her head covered with blood lying on the dashboard. He heard only faint groaning from her.

Dr. Brewer looked wildly around. "Eli! Eli!" he called out.

"Right here, Doc."

"Tell Ted Shutter to bring his stake bed truck around. We've got to get these people into my office right now!"

## 15

D r. George Brewer somberly looked at the receipt for the three bodies, while the morgue driver closed the rear door of the wagon. After securing the doors, they turned and waved wearily before going forward into the truck's cab. Doc spun slowly around towards his office. Lucy, her arms crossed, stood, leaning against the door frame within the entrance.

"Tough break, Doc," she said, looking remorseful.

"Yeah. Can't win 'em all," He replied sadly as he lowered the paper to his side before glancing west as the sun began making its retreat. Dr. Brewer scanned Lucy's shoes. "You think you can walk in the woods in those?"

"What do you mean?"

"Oh, I guess I was thinking out loud. What I meant to ask was, do you want to go for a ride in the country?"

"What does that have to do with my shoes?"

"You have to forgive me, Lucy. I'm not thinking straight. I was considering going out to Chinamans Bluff, and I wanted some company. I only mentioned your shoes because there's some walking involved."

Lucy smiled. "Sure, after today, I could use a break."

Dr. Brewer moved toward the entrance, and Lucy retreated inside and held the door open for him. She pointed at her shoes. "I figured I was going to be standing a lot on my feet today, so I wore these Oxfords. They're perfect for work, and I guess walking, too."

Doc's melancholy began to slowly evaporate. He looked down on his blood-spattered white coat. "Good, but before we leave, I have to clean up a bit."

A DARK, misty silhouette of Chinamans Bluff appeared intermittently between breaks in the forest as Dr. Brewer, and Lucy Lareau closed in on its secluded location. The rumble of the car and the cracking clatter of gravel beneath its undercarriage made conversation difficult, but Lucy feeling the need asked, "Why do they call this place Chinamans Bluff?"

Dr. Brewer kept his eyes trained on the narrow trail ahead. "I posed that same question when I first arrived in Chandlers Bend. I got two stories, and I suspect, over time, the locals melded both together. The first one says that a Chinaman set up camp at the base of the bluff. The second anecdote involves its shape. From a distance and specific location, the outline of the bluff resembles a Chinaman's cap with its round top."

"I thought the Chinese only worked out West?"

"Well, according to the locals, one made his way East—got this far and set up camp. He eked out a living doing laundry and other odd jobs for a time."

"You said for a time. What happened to him?"

"Funny, you asked the same questions that I did. Like many of the Chinese that stayed in this country, discrimination forced him to move on. I was told he went to New York City."

"Wow!" Lucy exclaimed. "I'm guessin' this burg doesn't like strangers, which makes me think I'll be run out of town on a rail, too."

"Don't worry, not every stranger gets the tar and feather treatment," said Dr. Brewer, looking at Lucy briefly and forcing a smile.

The road became uneven, and Lucy grabbed the front dashboard to steady herself as the car swayed within the furrows of previous tracks. "How much farther," she asked.

Before he could answer, the canopy of the overgrowth opened, and Lucy gazed at the towering side of the sandstone bluff. "Wow!" Lucy said as she strained her neck upward. She looked at him. "We're not going to up there, are we? You said a walk, not mountain climbing."

Dr. Brewer gave her a playful glance. "Why sure. It's not as rough as you think. This is the steep side. Come on. We'll go around to the other part," he said and sprung out of the car.

Lucy got out of the car cautiously and followed. Trailing behind Doc, she agilely stepped over fallen branches and an assortment of clumps of sandstone that littered the ill-defined trail. Doc's pace was broken only by an occasional pause urging her to keep up. Once they reached the other side, Lucy thought that a climb to the top of the bluff wasn't going to be as easy as he said. She regarded the sloping embankment and irregular outcroppings with apprehension. "How many girls have you taken on this trip and lived to tell about it?" asked Lucy, still gawking at the skyward challenge.

Doc laughed. "You're the first," he said and began to move upward along a narrow trail.

"Okay, but the soles on my shoes aren't exactly made for climbing."

Dr. Brewer paused and reached out to Lucy. "Come on, I'll help you." He offered her a hand. "Stay close to me, I know the secret path. We'll be on top in no time."

To Lucy's surprise, the jaunt to the summit wasn't as bad as she had imagined it would be. "Wow! What a nice view," she said, breathing heavily while marveling at the sight. She gazed in amazement at the large swaths of forest that had been cleared by eager loggers, and the amber glow of the sun as it hovered over the horizon. She moved cautiously, a few feet shy of the edge.

Doc, already at the rim of the bluff, squatted down and let his legs hang freely on the lip of the sandstone floor. He leaned back and propped himself against his elbows.

"If it's all the same to you," Lucy began, still enthralled at the scenery, "this is as close I care to get for now." She stopped a little way off to the side of Doc, but short of being able to extend her legs over the side. Lucy tucked her dress under her while carefully sitting down on the ground. She drew her legs toward her, hugging them with both arms.

"I come here when I want to think," Dr. Brewer said, staring out toward the horizon.

Lucy looked at his meditative profile. "Then, why did you want me along?"

"Today, I wanted to talk to someone else besides myself."

"Because of the car accident?"

"That's part of it. Everything I do is dissected and viewed under a microscope in this town. I really don't have a true confidant that I can trust."

"Not even a girlfriend?"

Dr. Brewer looked at Lucy. "Not even a girlfriend," he said regretfully, before turning back.

"Did you know any of those people that got ..." Lucy trailed off.

"Nope," he answered without looking at her. "From the information gathered at the scene, one was from the county seat, the other two, people from a town in Minnesota. I don't remember the name of the town, but I'm sure the news of their death will be a big shock to its residents. This kind of thing is big news in these small towns."

Lucy cleared her throat. "Doc, I don't mean to pry, but I'm just curious. Did you ever have a girlfriend?"

"Yeah, before the war. When I came back, she had other interests."

"I'm sorry to hear that."

"Don't be. Better early than later," he said sullenly. "It's a story as old as the hills. A guy goes off to fight the war and comes back, and things aren't the same. Either she's unfaithful, or he is, or he comes back with some psychological or physical damage. It rarely is back the same as before."

Lucy stroked her dress. "Ah... I wasn't nosing around in your things Doc, but I came across a Distinguished Service Cross commendation letter in your files. It had your name on it."

Dr. Brewer scratched the back of his neck. "It's nothing. It's just something the government gives to soldiers who are lucky enough to survive the war."

"I think it's more than that, Doc."

"Well, I'd rather not talk about it. And I think it's time for me to ask you a few questions."

Lucy shifted in place and looked at him uneasily. "Like what?"

"Like, how you ended up here?"

"Not much to say. I worked in the Windy City, got tired of looking at the lake, and hot-footed it up north to Wisconsin. I'm supposed to meet someone here."

"A guy?"

"Yeah, a guy," Lucy quipped. "I don't know when he's gonna show. So, rather than go stir crazy, I'd thought I would look for a job."

He smiled. "I'm glad you came along because I've got a lot of stuff that needs sorting."

"You don't have to tell me," Lucy joked. "I don't mean to change the subject, but that sun is getting pretty low. I'm guessin' you don't have a flashlight."

Dr. Brewer nodded. He turned on his side and pushed himself up before extending a hand toward Lucy. "C' mon, let's get going."

Little was said during their descent. By the time they reached the car, the sun had already disappeared behind the treeline.

Dr. Brewer started the car, turned on the lights, and cautiously retraced his way out of the forest, keeping it in second gear. When the car moved onto the gravel road, the ride became more comfortable, and he opened up the engine. "I suppose Helen Spencer is preparing supper for you tonight?" he asked while remaining focused on the road ahead.

"Yeah, it's part of the rent."

"Do you like living there?"

"I do. We went out for a couple of drinks the other day. She seems like a really nice gal. You're single, and she's single. I'm surprised you two never got together."

"I don't know about Helen's feelings, but as I said before, people in this town like to gossip. I don't want to add to that."

"Funny, she feels the same way about this town. You two would make a great pair."

"Speaking about gossip," Dr. Brewer began, "you don't care for Ida, my housekeeper, do you?"

Lucy smiled. "As a matter of fact, I don't. And I have a feeling that it's mutual. She's one of those town busybodies that Helen and I talked about. Why do you ask?"

"Being a doctor, one develops a sense about people, and I sorta got that impression. The reason my office is in such a state of turmoil is that I don't want Ida snooping around in there. I told her that's the only place she doesn't have to clean. And you can see, I haven't been too good at doing that."

"Leave it to me, Doc."

"Good. There's a lot of confidential information in that room needs to stay in that room, if you get my drift."

"I understand," Lucy said as she observed the long shadows of the tall pines slowly fade and merge with the approaching evening.

## 16

E li Buchanan, his shotgun trained toward the floor, walked into the Farmers & Mercantile Bank manager's office.

Bill Larsen looked up. "Expecting trouble today after hearing the news about Dillinger and his gang?" he asked uneasily, his eyes focused on the gun.

"I'm not going to take any chances. I'll be sittin' in my car on the sidestreet today. I got Henry Blake posted across the street again, on the second floor."

Larson nodded. "I think the Dillinger Gang is getting too close for comfort."

"That's why I'm still hanging around. I'm sure every lawman and bank owner in Wisconsin is also concerned." Eli Buchanan took a seat on the other side of Larsen's desk and rested the Winchester on his lap.

"Eli, you can count me among their number."

"Bill, I figured as much, but I personally don't think we have to worry too much. My guess they'll be heading for Chicago. I think every highway patrol officer and county sheriff is going to be on the lookout for them. That makes any of the state highways too hot for them to travel on."

"Why do you say that?"

Eli pointed to the map of Wisconsin that hung on Larson's wall. "Hey, following that shootout in Saint Paul, I doubt they'll be heading back that way. And after that gun battle in Manitowish Waters," Eli directed his attention to the lower right-hand section, "I'm guessing Chicago—because it's a big town with a lot of hiding places."

"So, you think they are going to come through our town to get there?"

"Don't really know for certain," Eli said. Shaking his head pensively, he rose. Keeping his right hand on the gun, he indicated with the other. "See, as I said, Dillinger and his gang will probably stay off the major highways." Eli traced his finger along one of the major arteries. "He'll pick the backroads." He waved his hand with uncertain emphasis over the web of crisscrossing routes.

Larson eased back into his chair. "Rumor has it that the gang broke up and everyone went their separate ways, So, there may not even be a gang anymore."

"You may be right, but I'm going to hang around the bank, just in case. You know the FBI labeled Dillinger 'Public Enemy Number One' and placed a $10,000 reward on his head."

"So, is it our safety or the money that holds your interest?" Larson asked with a hint of sarcasm.

Eli, outwardly unruffled, but fumed at the inference, let out a dismissive laugh. "Hey, Bill, if I do capture Dillinger, I'll deposit the reward money in your bank."

Bill Larsen answered with a wry smile and rose from his chair. "I'll walk you to the door, Eli."

"Don't bother. I found my way in, and I think I can find my way out."

As Eli descended the bank's stairs, he glanced across the street to the second-floor apartment. He gave Henry Blake a wave, which he countered with a tap of his index finger along the brim of his hat.

It was a chilly April morning under a cloudless sky. Eli grasped the open collar flap on his coat, closed it, and turned off Main Street to the sidestreet bordering the bank. His 1931 Buick Coupé was blanketed within the shadow from a west-facing building, depriving him of the sun's early morning rays and its warmth. He opened the car's door and rested the barrel of his shotgun against the passenger's side window before taking his place behind the wheel. Wanting to take the chill out, he started the car. Eli grabbed his Thermos bottle off the passenger side seat. He unscrewed the lid, pulled at the cork stopper, and poured some hot coffee into its metal cup. Recapping the bottle, Eli discreetly removed a pint of brandy from an inside coat pocket and poured some of its contents into the steaming brew. He slipped the bottle under the seat.

Dreamy eyed, Eli began to think of Lucy Lareau while gradually sipping his coffee. There was something in her manner that he found attractive. She was sharp, funny, and down-to-earth. Since his wife divorced him years ago, he never fostered a romantic interest. Now, after meeting Lucy, he began to entertain that possibility. It was a new sensation, one he was sure he never had, even with his first wife. He smiled in his reflection and began to think of ways to further a relationship with her.

Eli returned to the reality of the situation and intuitively blew over the cup and studied the morning's comings and goings of the town's inhabitants. He leaned back in his seat, lulled into a self-assurance that the Farmers & Mercantile Bank of Chandlers Bend was safe from armed robbers. He was startled by the unexpected approach of Olive Perkins, who tapped on his side window. Taken by surprise, Eli spilled some of his drink as he turned to his left.

"Hey, Eli," Olive Perkins yelled in an apparent attempt to be heard through the door's glass.

Annoyed, he placed his coffee on the floor away from Olive's prying eyes and sensitive nose and reluctantly rolled down his window. "What can I do for you today, Olive?"

"Hanging around the bank because of the Dillinger Gang?" she asked, her face revealing some delight.

"I'm not taking any chances. It's just a precaution."

"You gonna stay here all day?"

Wishing she would leave him alone, he said sharply, "I should be keeping an eye on the bank. I'm sure—"

The piercing ring of the bank's alarm broke off their conversation. Eli lunged for the shotgun. He grabbed the door's handle and pushed Olive backward onto the pavement. The noise of a muffled shot reached Eli's ears as he rounded the corner toward the bank's entrance. The few people who happened to be walking down the street stopped and gawked at the bank. When Eli came around the corner, holding his gun, they began to scatter and seek cover.

Crouching slightly, Eli pulled the pump action on the Winchester and injected a shell into its chamber. A man wearing an opened, somewhat dirty, brown work jacket, a light blue shirt, and bib coveralls emerged from the bank's front door. He was holding a pistol. Eli fired wildly. The casement on the door exploded in a shower of wood and glass fragments. Stunned, the man turned and trained his gun on Eli. Henry Blake, from his position across the street, fired his rifle. The man staggered backward and collapsed at the top of the stairs.

Eli drove another round into his shogun. Townspeople, hearing the discharge of gunfire, began to gather along Main Street. Albert Miller opened the front door of his grocery store to see what was going on before Mable Miller pulled him back to safety.

Another man, dressed in a soiled, tan drover's duster, came out of the bank and moved quickly over his partner's body. He pointed his double-barreled shotgun at Henry Blake's elevated position and returned fire. Blake, appearing to sense the man's actions, ducked below the window sill seconds before the gun's double-aught pellets sprayed his location. The gunman turned menacingly toward Eli. Before he was able to fire the other barrel, Eli shot the man in his stomach. The force of the impact pushed him back into the bank. From inside, Eli heard a chilling scream.

Along with the acrid smell of burnt gunpowder, the continual shrill of the bank's alarm heightened the tension.

Eli, his knees unsteady, held his position, uncertain how many robbers were still inside. His hands damp with perspiration and body shaking with adrenaline, he yelled, "Come out with your hands in the air!"

The incessant clang of the bank's alarm added to the throbbing in Eli's ears.

"Eli! It's me, Evelyn," she shouted over the hammer of the bell. "I'm coming out. Mr. Larsen's been shot."

From his post across the street, Blake shouted. "Eli! Eli ... the car behind you. Stop it!"

The intended getaway car, a four-door blue Chevrolet sedan with Minnesota plates, began to move and speed away. Wavering between acting on the news of Bill Larsen's unknown condition and the fugitive's car, Eli turned and fired at the fleeing vehicle. Its rear window disintegrated in an eruption of glass.

A few Chandlers Bend residents, who previously withdrew during the commotion, began to edge back into the building and take cover. Blake, from his vantage point, leaned precariously out of the window. Aiming unsteadily at the car, he fired without apparent effect.

Eli yelled to Henry Blake, "Take care of the bank!" He rushed to his still idling car, pushed in the shotgun's safety button, and threw it onto the passenger side. Putting the car in gear, he made a sharp turn onto Main Street and sped after his quarry. The car's straight-eight engine thundered under the pressure of Eli's foot on the accelerator. Eli knew that his one hundred-four horsepower engine could easily outpace the Chevrolet's six-cylinder sedan.

Rounding the curve and violently bouncing over the railroad tracks, Eli caught a glimpse of the blue car heading north, in the direction of Chinamans Bluff. Eli turned north without thinking about the possibility of crossing into traffic, his foot heavy on the gas peddle. Roaring along the straightaway, he reached for his Winchester. Precariously transferring the shotgun from one hand to the next, he struggled to maintain control. Eli awkwardly maneuvered the weapon through the window. Fighting the road's wind and unevenness, he rested the gun barrel on the spare tire secured to the left side of the engine's cowling.

Now within fifty feet of the fleeing car, Eli maneuvered his Buick Coupé to the right side of the road. Stones from the gravel sputtered against the car's body. The Chevrolet lurched left, and Eli pulled the trigger. The car's rear taillight shattered—the license plate dangled freely in the air. Eli pulled in the shotgun and pumped in his last round while fighting to control the vehicle. As he approached a bend, a Ford stake bed truck swerved into his lane, nearly forcing Eli off the road. Unnerved by the near-collision, Eli pushed hard on the gas peddle. Again he fought the wind and stiff resistance of the steering wheel. With an unsteady hand, he rested his gun on the spare tire again. The roadway angled upward, and the car roared, closing the gap between vehicles. Directing his attention on the left tire, Eli fired. The Chevrolet started to fishtail.

Eli eased back and drew in the shotgun. The sedan began to skid. The driver, appearing to overcorrect the vehicle, caused it to spin out of control. As it turned into the oncoming lane's shoulder, the car hit a ditch with such force that it began to roll over before careening down a steep embankment. Reaching the bottom of the slope, it smashed into a tree. With its exposed undercarriage, the getaway car's wheels spun as steam gushed from its overheated radiator.

Eli's car screeched to a halt. Quickly drawing his revolver, he jumped out of his car and ran across the highway. Eli kept his gun trained on the Chevrolet while moving closer. As he approached the driver's side of the upturned vehicle, he saw the partially decapitated, blood-soaked body of the driver sprawled near the wreck. In addition to the deceased, a couple of open suitcases were lying about—their contents littering the scene. Eli returned his gun to its holster before walking to the dead man. His hand, shaking, retrieved the man's wallet. He flipped it open and noticed only a few dollars inside but no identification. Eli put it into his coat pocket.

Eli crouched down and examined the interior of the vehicle. Several articles of clothing were strewn about—loose bullets, a shotgun, and a black satchel. He reached for the bag. After a brief struggle with the catch, it finally yielded, exposing piles of money— each unmarked pack neatly banded. Mulling over the opportunity for an immediate fortune, he considered the consequences. Eli, feeling trapped in a job no one wanted, a town full of memories, and the topic of rumor mongers, gazed broodingly upon his deliverance.

A car door slammed shut from the roadway above.

Eli, determined at making a change in his life, hastily grabbed several of the packets. He shoved them into the inside pockets of his three-quarter coat and snapped the bag closed, and set it aside. Eli pulled out his pocket notebook, and with a trembling hand, jotted down the number of the battered license plate.

## 17

Andy Voss, the county sheriff's deputy, approached and gave Eli a questioning look. Eli spotted the lawman's right hand hovering over his holstered revolver. "It's all over, Andy," Eli said, his voice flat with exhaustion. He detected the deputy's eyes drift from Eli's badge to the pouch.

"Our office got a call about the robbery. When we got word of it, Sheriff Dawson and I went to Chandlers Bend in separate vehicles. From what I saw, you left quite a mess."

"Besides the robbers, was anyone else killed?" Eli asked.

"Don't know. Dawson reckoned you'd need some help. So, here I am," the deputy said, still showing interest in the bag Eli held. "Whatcha got there?" he asked, nodding toward the black satchel.

Lifting the bag slightly, Eli said, "This?"

"Yeah."

"I suspect money the gang stole from one of their bank jobs."

"Whatcha going to do with it?" Deputy Voss asked, his tone distrusting.

"Count the money, file a report, and check with Minnesota authorities about their capture ... I mean death and see who the money belongs to."

Voss licked his lower lip. "How much do ya figure is in there?"

"A few thousand. I don't know—haven't counted it."

Moving closer to Eli, the deputy spoke in a hushed tone. "By rights, it should be divided between our departments."

Ignoring the comment, Eli hurried past the deputy and returned to his car.

From below, Deputy Voss called out to Eli. "What about that?" He pointed toward the wreck.

Eli opened his car door and threw the black bag onto the floor of the passenger's side. He looked back at the deputy. "I have to get going. I'll tell Dawson where you are when I see him."

Once Eli started for town, he reached under his seat and, with a shaking hand, found the pint bottle of brandy. He took a couple of deep gulps before replacing it. His thoughts wandered back to the shooting. It was the second time he ever killed someone. Eli knew, like the first time, it never would be erased from his memory.

THE COUNTY CORONER'S CAR, the county sheriff's car, and a black Dodge hearse surrounded the bank. Inside this cordon of vehicles, folks moved about, each absorbed in some official task.

When Eli pulled up, he was immediately surrounded by the curious. "Did he get away?" someone asked.

Seeing the crowd gather around Eli's car, Olive Perkins tried to push her way into the maelstrom of the curious. "Eli!" she yelled over the chatter of the throng.

As Eli opened the car door, he gave Olive Perkins a sullen nod. He met her at the edge of the gathering. He was holding the black satchel. "Olive, I can't say anything right now. I've got to check with Sheriff Dawson first." Brushing past her, Eli moved toward the bank.

"Okay, Eli, but I want an exclusive," Olive Perkins shouted.

Eli frowned and gave her an indifferent wave.

Sheriff Dawson stood in the shattered doorway at the top of the bank's set of steps. Looking somber, he called out, "Eli, come on up."

An antagonistic relationship existed between Eli and county sheriff, Frank Dawson. Part of the tension was a result of the war and Dawson's exemption from the draft. Appointed by his friend, the governor, after the death of the previous sheriff, he claimed his position was critical to the community's safety. When the time came for the regular election, Dawson, already deeply entrenched in the political machine, easily won.

Those circumstances alone were grounds for resentment, but while Eli was fighting overseas, Dawson and Eli's wife, Barbara, became involved. Although the two of them weren't blatant in the affair, those kinds of things were hard to keep a secret when the gossip of the townsfolk's comings and goings were favorite pastimes. The rumor of the scandal rankled the sensibilities of the community, and the news rivaled the war. Some people speculated on Eli's reaction when he returned home. None of their predictions ended well, yet when Eli returned, he appeared to have stuffed his anger by taking to drinking as a solution.

Eli nodded once and avoided eye contact. He offered the bag of money to Dawson. "Frank. I got this from the getaway car. I haven't counted it."

"I gather the driver is dead?"

Eli stepped gingerly around the blood-spattered entrance and focused his attention on the interior of the bank. "Yeah, killed when his car went off the road—a couple of miles north of Chinamans Bluff. I heard a gunshot coming from the bank just before the alarm went off. Was anyone else killed?"

Sheriff Dawson followed Eli. Dawson pointed toward the bank owner's office door. "Bill Larsen got a flesh wound to his left shoulder. Doc Brewer's treating him now in his office. He's lucky—nothing serious."

"What about Evelyn Ferris? She called out to me toward the end. I guess she's okay?"

"Yeah, she's all right—just a bit shook. Mrs. Ferris is in the back room with her husband. She didn't want to leave because the bank wasn't secured," Dawson said.

Eli placed the satchel down on a nearby table, emptied his pocket of the getaway driver's wallet, and pulled out his notebook. "Any idea who these guys are?"

Dawson shook his head. "I haven't had a chance to check their personal belongings. I suspect we'll learn more after we examine the car."

"I did jot down the license plate number," Eli said, looking at his open notebook. "It's from Minnesota, but knowing criminals, the car's probably stolen."

Dawson retrieved the wallet and spread it open. Running a thumb over the money, he said, "Nothing but cash in here." He set it back down. "We need to count the money, but before that, we should get a witness. I'll see if Evelyn Ferris wants to help us."

Evelyn's husband, Bill, accompanied Dawson. "My wife's too upset right now, but if it's okay, I can witness the count."

Finished counting, Sheriff Dawson and Eli signed the acknowledgment of $6,546. Bill

Ferris confirmed it, and Evelyn Ferris, obviously still distraught, placed it in the bank's safe.

Sheriff Dawson motioned toward a chair. "Evelyn, if you are up to it, can you tell us what happened during the robbery?"

She sat down and looked somberly at Dawson. "It all happened so quickly."

"Hold on for a minute," Eli said. "I want to get Olive Perkins. She'll be wanting to hear this, and I don't want to have to repeat it."

Olive, keeping a vigil outside, eagerly came in and sat down on a nearby chair, her pencil and notebook at the ready. Eli gave the nod for Evelyn to go-ahead.

"These two men came in here shortly after you left, Eli. The shorter one starts walking toward my window. We never saw either of those two men before. So, Mr. Larsen asks, 'What can I do for you, gentlemen?'"

"'A lot!' the man shouts. Then he says, 'This is a stick-up! One false move and I'll fill yah full of holes.'" Evelyn took a handkerchief and dabbed her eyes. "Mr. Larsen comes by me and pushes me aside.

He starts collecting money from my cash drawer then steps on the floor alarm button. The man yells, 'Wiseguy, eh?' He turns his gun towards Mr. Larsen, but his revolver hits one of the bars on the teller's cage, and it fires. Fearing for my life, I fell to the ground and ducked under the counter. I see Mr. Larsen also lying down, squirming in pain, with blood on his shoulder. I didn't know how serious it was. I thought he was going to die. After that, I don't know. All I heard was the shooting coming from outside."

Eli looked at Bill Perkins. "I think you should take your wife home. The safe is secured. I'll make sure the door gets boarded up until it's fixed. She's been through a lot today."

When Olive was alone with Eli, she got his account of the chase.

"Well, Eli, this is the most exciting thing that has happened in this town since the *Great Fire of 1917*," Olive said, arrogantly folding her notebook and placing it into her purse.

"You're lucky to be alive and able to report this story, Olive."

"I know that, and tomorrow's edition is certainly going to cover my narrow escape from death," she said boastfully. Cheerful, she left the bank, deftly stepping around the bloodstained entrance.

Eli's gaze followed her descent until she faded from view. His eyes wandered back to the discolored floor as he rebuttoned his coat. He felt the bulk from the money on his chest as well as on his conscience.

## 18

"Here's your papers, Vincent," Olive Perkins said. "I've given you twenty-five more copies than usual. I'm confident people will want more—after all, it not every day the *Farmers & Mercantile Bank* gets robbed." She presented him with a voucher to sign.

Vincent "Fudge" Spencer obediently signed then hesitated in returning the pencil. "Mrs. Perkins," he began timidly, "would you autograph my copy of the newspaper?"

Olive Perkins beamed. "Why, of course, Vincent. I'd be delighted." She plucked the pencil from Vincent's outstretched hand, and with great flourish, signed her name across the newspaper's banner headline. "There," she said, "hang on to that, Vincent, it may be worth some money when you get older."

Vincent accepted the paper and looked affectionately at her. "Someday, when I'm a reporter, I'll frame this and hang it in my office."

Olive Perkins chuckled. "Who knows, Vincent, but for now, you need to get those papers delivered."

He nodded, slung the bag over his shoulder, and quickly left the loading area.

Having dispensed most of his papers, Vincent stopped at the barbershop. There were more than the usual amount of customers crammed into its small interior. Louis Girard stood, engaged in trimming Bill Larsen's already short-cropped hair, while the latter held court.

Girard greeted Vincent. "Maître Fudge, at last, zee paper." He reached out and snatched the newspaper from Vincent's already obeying hand.

"Hey, Fudge, gimme one of them papers, too," Bill Larsen demanded from his royal roost. "I want to make sure Olive Perkins spelled my name correctly."

A wave of laughter echoed throughout the shop.

"Mr. Larsen, I've already delivered a copy to your house," said Vincent clumsily.

"Fudge, it's not every day that you get shot. By now, Mrs. Larsen probably wore off the print on that copy already just reading it." Larsen reached into his pants pocket. "Here's a nickel. Hand it to me."

"I'd like a copy, too," someone else said. In rapid succession, Vincent satisfied the demand for more copies.

As Vincent made the rounds among the men, Bill Larsen exuberantly rehashed his story. "Look at this headline." He raised the paper in the air. "'BANK ROBBERS SHOT DEAD,'" he bellowed—his bravado suggesting some involvement in the actual slayings. "Now, ain't that the truth."

Another round of unworried laughter filled the shop.

While listening to Mr. Larson's account, it wasn't long before Vincent lightened the load in his newspaper bag—leaving with an additional forty-five cents in his pocket.

Breathlessly arriving into his mother's kitchen, he managed to shout, "Extree! Extree! Read all about it, Mom."

Vincent proudly waved the newspaper in the air. "Mrs. Perkins wrote about yesterday's bank robbery, and she signed my copy, too. I wish I'd been there to see all the action."

Helen Spencer paused from stirring the stew she was preparing for the evening meal. With unusual sadness etched in her eyes, she looked at Vincent. "When you get older, you'll understand that killing isn't something to be excited about."

"I didn't mean anything by it, Mom. I just thought it would have been exciting to see a real bank robbery."

"Well, as your mother, I'm just glad you were in school at the time. Now, leave the paper on the cabinet and get ready for supper. After you wash up, go upstairs and tell Miss Lareau that we are about ready to eat."

Dispirited by the rebuke, Vincent said sullenly, "Sure, Mom," and headed for the bathroom.

He washed hurriedly, and taking two steps at a time, rushed upward to the second floor. The door to Lucy Lareau's room was ajar. Vincent caught a glimpse of her legs positioned at the foot of her bed, with one leg slightly drawn up toward her. He timidly knocked.

"Come in," she said invitingly.

Vincent stepped into the room and found Lucy Lareau resting on her bed, dressed only in her slip and bra. "Oh, I'm ... I'm sorry," he sputtered. He immediately looked down at the floor in embarrassment. "My mom said that supper will be ready soon."

Lucy giggled. "Thanks, Vincent. Tell your mom I'll be right down."

Red-faced, he turned and went across the hall into his room and quickly closed the door. He felt his heart pounding. Although no longer in the presence of Miss Lareau, his retention of her reclining in such an alluring pose remained. Despite his fixation, he briefly held up the newspaper and gave the headline an appreciative look before leaving it on his dresser.

When he opened his door, he heard a rustling of fabric from inside Miss Lareau's room. Still, in the fantasies of adolescent desires, he quietly headed downstairs for the evening meal.

"Is Miss Lareau coming?" Vincent's mother asked.

"Yes, Mom," he answered distantly.

She eyed him. "Everything okay?" she asked. "You were chipper moments ago."

Vincent took his place at the kitchen table. "I'm all right, Mom. I think I'm a little tired after all the excitement of delivering today's paper."

The drum of Lucy Lareau's footsteps drew closer from the stairwell. Coming into view, she gave Vincent a playful smile.

He shifted uncomfortably in his chair.

"I didn't get a chance to talk with you, Miss Lareau. You came in so suddenly and rushed upstairs before I could even say anything. I suppose work wasn't as hectic as yesterday's," Helen Spencer asked as she placed the bowl of stew on the table.

"Oh, it was busy enough," Lucy Lareau said, helping herself to a slice of bread. "There were a bunch of reporters asking a lot of questions about the robbery. Some came from as far away as Milwaukee."

"My Vincent, here, is going to be a reporter someday," Helen said boastfully, smiled, and gazed approvingly at her son.

"Is that so?" Lucy Lareau commented. "Why, I think you'd make a great reporter."

Vincent felt a sense of relief, fearful that Miss Lareau might say something about the awkward encounter earlier upstairs. "Yes, and I've been following the activities of the Dillinger Gang ... I have all the newspaper clippings," he said boastfully, his voice rising slightly.

"What about the Barrow Gang? Have you been following them, too?" Lucy asked.

"Yes, I have, Miss Lareau. I've been following the news about all the gangs."

"Vincent, I think that's enough talk about criminals," Helen Spencer said, then turned her attention to Lucy Lareau. "You began telling us about your day."

Lucy displayed some hesitancy. "It has something to do with the robbery."

Helen let out a nervous laugh. "Oh, I suspect the talk in town will be about the robbery for some time. I just didn't want Vincent to give us the latest news of every criminal in the country." She gave her son a wink.

"As I said, reporters came to visit Doctor Brewer. Olive Perkins was among them. They asked him about Bill Larsen and how badly he was wounded."

"Mr. Larsen said he escaped certain death by knocking the gun away as the bank robber shot at him," Vincent muttered, his mouth full of stew.

"Vincent, don't talk with your mouth full," Helen ordered. "Miss Lareau, how badly was he injured?"

"Well, from what I saw, there was more blood than much of a wound. But, I'm sure Bill doesn't see it that way."

Helen joined Lucy in laughter.

"Did anyone say who the bank robbers were?" asked Helen.

Lucy shook her head. "At the time, I'm not sure anyone knew, but I bet it will be in this evening's paper."

Helen motioned toward the kitchen counter. "I haven't had a chance to look at it yet."

The newspaper was within reach. Lucy grabbed it and briefly scanned the top fold. "It says it was two brothers, Caleb and Si Johnson. It says here that the third man, the driver was..." She flipped the paper over and froze.

"Miss Lareau, are you all right?" asked Helen.

Suspended in mid-action, Lucy stared at something on that page.

Vincent saw his mother look at Lucy with concern.

"Miss Lareau?" asked Helen.

Lucy Lareau returned the paper to the counter, pushed her chair back, and abruptly rose. "You'll have to excuse me. I don't feel so good."

## 19

E li considered the pile of money strewn on his bed. He ran his fingers through the loose bills and felt a rush of ecstasy tempered with contrition. Eli guessed the amount to be somewhere between four and five thousand dollars. His estimate was solely based on volume because it nearly matched the size he and Sheriff Dawson counted. Although the shade was closed, he nervously checked his window.

*It's the criminal's money. Where did they get it?*

Burying his conscience under the stack bills, he began to count and sort his trove by denomination. To help steady his hands, Eli fortified himself with a couple of swings of brandy. He set the bottle down on the nightstand. With the piles in neat rows, he counted each and labeled their totals on small slips of paper. When finished, Eli tallied each pack and entered the various sums onto a sheet of notepaper. He laid back on the bed alongside the money, raised the page over his head, and stared at the total—$5,275. Eli let go of the paper, and it drifted onto the floor.

Eli cupped his hands behind his head and closed his eyes. His mind wandered beyond the village limits of Chandlers Bend, mentally spending his ill-gotten wealth. His eyes drifted around his modest room. He hated the flowery wallpaper, the meager furnishings, and the bed that groaned every time he shifted on its uneven surface. Now in his state of contemplation, his small desk, worn armchair, and a tiny table with unmatched wooden chairs felt inadequate. Eli thought how great Prohibition had been for him and how he had money to spend. Now it was over. Now he had to live on the measly income of a town constable. *But that was before yesterday.*

There was a rustling noise from outside his door, quickly followed by a knock.

Eli hurriedly got up and quickly hid the money under his pillow. "Who's there?" he asked cautiously.

"Eli, it's Frank Dawson."

A rush of acid filled Eli's stomach. With his heart pounding, he moved toward the door and unbolted it. "What do you want, Frank?" Eli asked, widening the opening to his apartment.

"Your landlady let me in. I'd rather not talk in the hallway. May I come in?"

Eli waved the sheriff in. "I don't usually have any visitors. I only have one armchair, but if you don't mind sitting at my table."

Frank Dawson grabbed one of the chairs and sat down.

There was an awkward silence as Eli grabbed the other chair and sat across from Dawson.

Dawson opened up his jacket. He pulled out a small notebook and glanced down at it. "That getaway car, it was stolen from a farmer near Hastings, Minnesota. It was later used to rob a bank in that town."

"Was anybody killed?" Eli asked.

Dawson looked at him briefly and said coldly, "Yeah, a bank teller." He cleared his throat. "Based on the description of the robbers, it's believed the same gang was involved in the robbery of the Red Wing Merchants Bank three days later."

"Any idea who these guys were?"

"I'll tell you something, Eli. With these criminals, like the Dillinger and the Barrow Gang, robbing banks, everyone wants to get into the action. The newspapers are making these bums into heroes—some sort of Robin Hoods. Well, it appears that a pair of brothers teamed up with another no-good and decided to go into the bank-robbing business. They were Caleb and Si Johnson. You probably saw their names in the paper."

Eli shook his head. "I didn't. I've been trying to cope with the whole thing. Everybody wants to hear my story. It's too much for me right now."

Sheriff Dawson nodded. "Your first kill?" he asked matter-of-factly.

"No. The war. You don't forget."

Eli observed Dawson looking at the bottle on his nightstand.

"I know you don't like me, Eli, but take my advice. Uncorking a bottle isn't gonna help."

"Frank, you're right about my attitude toward you. While I was off fighting the war, you were jumping my wife. It's hard getting beyond that. Right now, as police officers, we gotta work together. I do my job, and you do yours—that's all that matters."

Dawson glanced around uneasily then looked back at Eli. "Okay, you're right. No matter what I say or do, it's not going to change anything. So, setting our differences aside, I'll tell you what I learned."

Eli gave Dawson a listless nod.

"Anyway, these two-bit hoodlums were local troublemakers from Hastings. They teamed up with another thug, Adam Schiller. He was their driver. These guys were not known for their intelligence." Dawson laughed. "Robbing a bank in your town isn't the smartest thing to do."

"Well, thanks for that information, but couldn't all this wait until tomorrow?"

"I reckon it could, but I thought you'd like to know that there may be a reward for their capture."

Eli stiffened and fell back against his chair.

"Yeah, I figured you'd react that way. After the death of the bank teller in Hastings, they put up a reward of one thousand dollars."

"Well, that certainly is good news, I mean, besides the death of the bank teller."

Sheriff Dawson's mood appeared to toughen. "There's just one problem."

"What's that?" Eli felt his heart race.

"The bank also wants its money back."

Eli crossed his arms over his chest. "How much did they lose?" he asked, his voice breaking.

Dawson pulled out a piece of paper from his shirt pocket. "$10,597."

Eli shifted uneasily in his chair. "What about the other bank?"

"They're not sure. The bank had some customers at the time, and the robbers took their money as well. They estimated about three-thousand in total."

Eli spotted the slip of paper that he used to figure the amount he recovered from the getaway car under the bed. A good portion of the note was visible and disclosed its use. Eli felt there was a tone of an accusation in Dawson's comment. He exclaimed, "You're not suggesting I had—"

"Hold on to your britches, Eli. I'm not suggesting anything," Dawson shouted. "I only said there's a lot of unaccounted money. Between the Hastings' haul and Red Wing, there's a little more than five grand that's missing."

Eli's face turned crimson, and he tried to recover from his anger. He cleared his throat and asked, "So, now what?"

"Well, for one thing, we're not splitting the money because we know who it belongs to. I've already contacted the banks and told them what we have recovered."

"What about the rest?"

Sheriff Dawson rose from his chair and started for the door. Eli, close behind, purposely blocked Dawson's view of the sheet of paper under Eli's bed.

"When my deputy and I searched the bodies," Dawson began, "the car, and of course the wallets, we found only a few hundred dollars. My guess, they probably hid some of the cash somewhere along the way between Red Wing and here."

"And the reward?"

Dawson laughed. "With all that money missing, maybe all you're gonna get is their thanks. But, who knows."

## 20

With her face buried deep into her pillow, Lucy Lareau sobbed bitterly. Heartbroken, the news of John Hamilton's death was too much of a shock. Anguished as she was over his killing by authorities, it was further agonizing to read that he had another girlfriend. When skimming the news of his death, the name Pat Cherrington cut deeply into Lucy's heart as well as the report of John's passing. Exhausted, torn between mourning and jealousy, she cried herself asleep.

Lucy awoke to the knocking at her door. The rising moon was barely lighting the interior as she looked at her bedside clock on the side table. It was at half-past seven.

Lucy answered drowsily, "Just a minute."

Brushing aside the hair from her face and straightening her crumpled dress, she walked over and cracked open her door. Helen stood at the top landing; the light from the bottom of the staircase illuminated her. Lucy could see the concern in Helen Spencer's eyes —worry for her wellbeing.

"Hi, Lucy," Helen said softly. "I only wanted to check if you were all right."

"I'm okay. I'm a dame who rolls with the punches," she said puckishly.

"Vincent is in his room, studying. Would you care to join me in the parlor for a glass of wine?"

Lucy briefly mulled over the offer. Coming out of her snit, she said, "Ya know, I think that's a swell idea. I could use a jolt of something, as long as it's got some kinda kick. Lead the way."

The parlor's only light came from a small lamp that rested on a writing desk near the front window. Lucy selected one of the two mismatched armchairs. Helen went to a curio cabinet, and from the lower portion, she removed a bottle of red wine that appeared nearly full. She held the bottle in Lucy's direction and said apologetically, "I save this for special occasions. I think tonight would be one of them."

Lucy nodded and surveyed the room.

Helen filled two glasses, hesitated before placing the bottle on a nearby table. She offered one of the drinks to Lucy. "I hope this helps," she said, giving the glass a slight lift.

Lucy accepted and toasted, "To your health."

Helen's glass met hers. They both took a sip of wine before Helen sat down in the adjoining chair. "I have to admit," Helen began, "I find your company refreshing after dealing with mill workers and railroad men."

"Thanks. Having spent most of my life in the big city, passing time in this burg is quite a change for me as well."

Helen looked wounded.

"Hey, Helen, don't get me wrong. It's just that I'm accustomed to a faster lifestyle."

Helen nodded. "I think I know what you mean. I'd like to have Vincent go to journalism school, but I honestly can't see that happening as long as we stay in Chandlers Bend. With the money I earn, it barely makes ends meet. And I insist the money Vincent earns delivering newspapers is his to save. I hope President Roosevelt will help turn things around."

Lucy downed her drink. "Do you suppose I could get a refill?" she asked unabashedly.

"Sure," Helen replied. She finished the rest of her drink before retrieving the bottle, this time portioning out a more generous serving.

Once back in her chair, Helen asked, "If you don't mind me asking, what upset you at supper?"

Lucy had anticipated the question long before she received the invitation to join Helen. She knew her reaction to reading the newspaper would raise some issues. Lucy purposely took another mouthful of wine to delay answering. "I think I've got the picture—my boyfriend isn't coming to meet me. It just hit me. That and the bank robbery was too much for me to deal with. The closeness of crime is troubling in itself. I felt abandoned and broke down—sorta like a jalopy without gas." Lucy smiled self-consciously. "I'm sorry if I upset you and Vincent."

"So, what are you going to do now? I mean, if he's not coming to get you..."

There was an uncomfortable silence as Lucy struggled for an answer. Finally, she said, "I don't have any relatives that I can live with." She stared blankly at the far wall.

After another protracted pause, Helen interrupted Lucy's pensive mood. "You could continue to stay here."

Lucy looked at Helen with surprise and felt eased by the suggestion. "Yeah, I guess I could do that," she said and held out her empty glass toward Helen.

"This month's Saturday night dance is coming up," Helen said while pouring the drink. "That should help take away the blues."

"Maybe," she answered indifferently. "And speaking of the dance, does Eli ever go to it."

"Moving on already, are you?" Helen asked with a wry smile.

"I had my cry. Remember, I'm the kind of gal who rolls with the punches."

Helen filled her glass, set the half-empty bottle aside, and resumed sitting. "As far as Eli, we've been friends for years, ever since grade school. I like him, and he's a pretty decent guy, but we never were romantically involved. He comes to the dance, not so much for the dancing, but more as a lawman. You know, once in a while, he needs to break up a fight."

"Why hasn't some gal latched on to him?"

Helen appeared to search for an answer. "I don't like to talk about Eli behind his back," she began slowly, "but Eli had a wife who chased around when he was fighting in the war. When he came back, he got divorced and began to hit the bottle. He's developed a little bit of a drinking problem."

"If you don't mind me saying, Helen, most of the people in this town appear to have a drinking problem."

Helen laughed. "You certainly got that right." She raised her nearly empty glass. "Maybe, tonight, that would include us."

"So, aside from his drinking and maybe some war issues, would you say he's okay?"

"You thinking of seeing him?"

"Maybe," Lucy said with a sheepish smile. "He is pretty handsome."

"He's one of my laundry customers. I'll see what I can do," Helen said with a wink.

"I'd appreciate that ... and do you suppose I could have one more fill?"

"Sure, Lucy, one more for the road."

They both broke out into spontaneous laughter.

## 21

E li looked up from his breakfast plate and noticed Beatrice Girard talking with a couple of strangers with their backs facing him. At first, he didn't give it much thought until Beatrice motioned toward him. When they turned and approached his table, their badges revealed they were lawmen. Both men wore rancher style hats and suits with vests. The taller of the two sported a grey Stetson, was muscular, and displayed a handlebar mustache. The shorter one was leaner, clean-shaven, and had a slight limp. He wore a black slouch hat.

"I understand you are Eli Buchanan," the taller one said while extending his hand.

With some uneasiness, Eli rose and returned the handshake. "Yeah, what can I do for you?"

"My name is Chester O'Neal. I'm the sheriff of Dakota County." He motioned to his partner. "This is Bryan Cobb. He's the sheriff of the neighboring Goodhue County, Minnesota."

With equal civility, Eli shook his hand. "I suppose you're here for the money."

Sheriff O'Neal nodded. "I see we're interrupting your breakfast."

"I'm guessin' you boys might want some grub, too?"

Sheriff Cobb spoke up. "We could use a bit of coffee and maybe some pie."

Eli motioned toward the chairs. "Have a seat, gentlemen. The coffee's good and the pie is excellent," he said and signaled to Beatrice.

While everyone placed their orders, Eli finished his breakfast. He took a sip of his coffee and cleared his throat. "The bank doesn't open until nine, so there is no rush."

"We've been on the road nearly three hours and could use the break," Sheriff O'Neal said. "It gives a chance to hear about your town's bank robbery."

"Yep," Sheriff Cobb began, "we heard from your county sheriff that it was quite a bloody mess."

Beatrice dropped off the order of pies and filled everyone's coffee cups. She lingered a bit before receiving a look of reproof from Eli.

Eli drew back against his chair. Hesitantly, he began. "I ... I was just sitting in my car, you know, keeping an eye on the bank, when the alarm went off. When I reached the front of the bank, one of the robbers starts coming out." Eli's voice faltered.

"Hey, I understand," Sheriff Cobb said softly. "I got this here limp from when I was in France. I know what it's like coming under fire."

Eli nodded appreciatively. "My deputy shoots him dead from across the street. Another guy comes out, and I fire." Eli pauses. "The next thing, my deputy calls out that the getaway car is leaving town. I fired my shotgun, knocking out his rear window, but he keeps going. I figured things were under control in town, so I jump into my car and haul after him."

"How long did all this take?" Sheriff O'Neal asked.

Shaking his head in hesitancy, Eli said, "I don't know, maybe five minutes."

"What kind of car were you driving that you were able to catch up with the getaway car?" Sheriff O'Neal asked.

"A 1931 Buick Coupé."

"Ha," Cobb laughed. "A straight eight against ... what was that again?"

"A Chevrolet six-cylinder sedan."

"No match," Cobb countered.

"Well, anyway, I got within, maybe twenty feet or so, and fired my last round. The car started to zigzag uncontrollably, I drew back, and it went off the road, crashing into a stand of trees at the bottom of a gulley."

"So, did you have a shootout?" asked Cobb impatiently.

"I got out of my car and drew my revolver, but the accident finished him off. I found him ejected from the car and decapitated."

Sheriff O'Neal and Cobb both sat back in their chairs. "Now, that's some story," declared O'Neal, slapping the table in approval.

Eli looked at his pocket watch. "The bank is about to open. Come on. It's just a short walk from here." He placed a dollar on the table and followed the two sheriffs out of the restaurant.

Once outside, Eli kept on the well-worn path over the railroad tracks that led to the center of town.

Bill Larson, his arm still in a sling, looked up guardedly as they entered the bank.

"Morning, Bill," Eli greeted. "These men are here to collect that stolen money."

"Morning," Bill Larson muttered. "I suppose we have to recount it?"

Evelyn Ferris was coming out of the vault. "Good morning, Eli," she said, her familiar lilt absent.

"Hiya, Evelyn," Eli said casually, preoccupied by Bill Larson's remark. "Well, that is standard procedure, Bill." He gestured, "This is Sheriff O'Neal and Sheriff Cobb. Sheriff O'Neal's from Hastings and Sheriff Cobb's from Red Wing—"

"Bill Larson," he interrupted, extending a welcoming hand. "Come on into my office, gentlemen." He ushered them through the adjacent caged teller's doorway and into his office. "Have a seat, gentlemen. Eli, I guess you'll have to stand. I'll be back in a minute with the money."

"Not much for conversation, is he?" Cobb remarked sarcastically.

"Yeah," Eli replied. "I forgot to mention that he was wounded during the robbery. He's playing the victim. From what I heard, he changes his tune in the barbershop—claims he confronted the robbers."

Sheriff O'Neal sat with one leg crossed over the other. His elbow rested on his right knee. "You'd think he'd be more grateful," he said, calmly stroking his mustache.

"Well, that's sort of his way, I guess," Eli countered.

Bill Larson returned, carrying a black leather bag in his hand. "Here it is, gentlemen," he said, eyeing the group with hesitancy. "How should we do this?"

O'Neal cleared his throat and rose. "I'll count, and you can verify the amount, Mr. Larson."

Following the counting of the money, Sheriff O'Neal reached inside his suit and pulled out an envelope. "I didn't want to say anything before, but there is the matter of a reward." He removed a folded sheet of paper and unfolded it on Larson's desk. "I've been instructed to present Eli with a reward of one thousand dollars. It's for the recovery of ... well, of some of the money. And, of course, the apprehension of the bank robbers. Eli, all I need is your signature."

Eli shifted uneasily in place. "I don't know what to say. I was just doing my duty."

O'Neal slid the paper toward Eli. From his other inside coat pocket, he drew out two banded packs of twenty-dollar bills. He laid them on top of the unsigned receipt. "Just sign, and we'll be on our way."

With a moist hand and fighting pangs of guilt, Eli accepted Sheriff O'Neal's ink pen and signed.

After returning O'Neal's pen, Eli grabbed the reward money and started to pocket it.

"Eli," Bill Larson uttered insistently, "that's a lot of money to be carrying around. Need I remind you of your promise to deposit reward money into my bank?"

Smirking, Eli quipped, "Bill, that was for the capture of the Dillinger Gang. Remember?"

O'Neal and Cobb glanced at each other.

Noting their air of puzzlement, he said, "It's a private joke, gentle-men." Eli slid the money back onto O'Neal's desk. "I'll come back later for my deposit slip, Bill."

With the legal proceeding completed, the trio gathered in front of the bank. "Thanks for the reward money," Eli said. "Our county sheriff told me about the reward. When he said that, I just figured, well, you know, the missing money... "

O'Neal shook his head. "The money isn't for the recovery of the loot. It's for taking care of the gang. The people of Hastings are pretty furious over the death of the bank teller. He was well-liked by the townsfolk. That money your banker friend took from you was from a collection we took from the citizens of Hastings. We better get going, Eli. Thanks for the coffee and pie."

"Anytime. If you ever come back to Chandlers Bend, stop in, and I'll treat you again."

Following a round of handshakes, Sheriff O'Neal and Sheriff Cobb started to leave. There was hesitation from O'Neal. He turned and said, "Eli, there's something I forgot to mention. I didn't want to say anything in front of Bill Larson."

"What's that?"

The three men once again drew closer.

"It's not a big issue. Nothing you really have to concern yourself with. I just thought you'd like to know." O'Neal moved nearer to Eli. "There were actually four members of the gang."

Eli felt a surge of uneasiness.

"Caleb Johnson had a girlfriend. When he left Hastings, she went with him. So, I guess she unknowingly became a member of the gang. After the bank teller's death, she became disenchanted with the life of crime, and she parted company with Caleb in Red Wing. From what she said so far, that was after the robbery of the bank in that town. The story she gave us was that she pleaded with Caleb to let her go when they left Red Wing. Well, they did—a few miles out of town. Caleb gave her several hundred dollars, and she hitched a ride back to Red Wing before taking a train back to Hastings. Her mother called us when her daughter got home."

Eli asked, "What else did she have to say?"

"Well, you know, these criminal types, ya got to weed through a lot of what they say," O'Neal said glibly.

Eli wanted to know more without appearing too concerned. "Now that the gang is eliminated, what do you think you can learn from her?" he asked matter-of-factly.

O'Neal laughed. "There's a sizable amount of money still missing. What she told us so far is that, other than the money she got from Caleb, the gang had all the loot from both bank jobs when they left Red Wing."

## 22

Back in his room, Eli mulled over his situation. He considered leaving town, but that would undoubtedly create suspicion. The unexpected news that the bank robbers had the fourth accomplice put him in an awkward position. If he confessed, it would mean prison. If he left, he would be pursued, captured, and ultimately sentenced to jail anyway. The thought occurred to him to return to the crash scene and scatter the money, but he knew it was too late to do that.

*I have to wait this out.*

Eli gathered the cash and put it into a small cloth bag, then stuffed it deep into his dresser's bottom drawer. He rearranged the contents to mask the money further. Momentarily satisfied with his decision, he took two large gulps of brandy to calm his frayed nerves.

He surveyed his room and caught a glimpse of the sheet of paper that he used to calculate his spoils. Eli promptly picked it up, crumpled the paper into a tight ball, and pitched it into his wastebasket. Once more, he looked around and found nothing to be concerned about and left to conduct his rounds.

In the hallway, Eli moved unhurriedly past his landlady. He saw in her eyes that she regarded him with some unease. "You okay, Eli? You're looking a little peaked."

"I'm fine, Mrs. Larpin. Maybe it's still the robbery."

"Aye, Lord knows what evil is out in this world."

He tipped his hat. "You have a great day, Mrs. Larpin."

"You, too, Eli. And may the good Lord keep you in the palm of his hand."

His landlady's remark echoed in his mind as he made his morning rounds. That and the compliments from fellow townsfolk left Eli in an angry mood that chewed at his gut.

Following his initial tour of Chandlers Bend, Eli made his way to Helen Spencer's house to pick up his laundry. He found Helen, with her back facing him, outside hanging clothes on the line.

"Good morning, Helen," Eli greeted listlessly.

Helen immediately turned and smiled. "You startled me. I guess I was deep in thought. Here to pick up your laundry?"

"Yeah. Feeling a little poorly today. I thought I get my stuff and go back to my room for a catnap."

"I don't know how you did what you did, but from what I hear, you're a hero in the eyes of many in this town."

Eli glanced briefly at the lawn before looking back at Helen. "I just happened to be in the wrong place at the right time."

"It's more than that, Eli. Anyway, give me a few minutes while I finish hanging these things."

"Take your time, Helen. I'm in no hurry."

Helen paused and meditatively held onto a clothespin secured to a fluttering bedsheet. "Hey, Eli," she began hesitantly, "you know that the monthly Saturday night dance is this weekend."

"Yep," he answered guardedly.

"Well ... I ... was just thinking if—"

"You asking me out, Helen?"

Blushing, she laughed. "Not exactly."

The worry he carried left him briefly. He teased, "Well, what exactly?"

"You can be such a pain at times."

"Helen, I'm sorry. I was just having some fun with you. After the … you understand. You're the only person in this town I feel at ease with and won't pester me about the bank robbery."

"Thanks, Eli. The feeling is mutual. What I wanted to say was Lucy is feeling a little sad lately. I suggested that she comes with me to the dance. I wondered if you would like to join us at our table and maybe ask her for a dance or two. I'm sure it would help lift her spirits?"

Eli smiled. "Who's idea was this, yours or Lucy's?"

"You're making this harder than I thought it would be. Yes or no?"

"I'll be there, but, isn't Lucy and Doc sort of keeping company?"

"As far as I know, it's only work connected."

"Well, in that case, you can count on me to be there."

"Good. Now I'll get your things so you can take your nap."

ELI ENTERED his room and checked to see if any of his belongings had been disturbed—mainly his ill-gotten money. Only his bed, which he left unmade, had been attended to by his landlady. Suspicion and paranoia were beginning to become part of his thinking. The worm of guilt gnawed at him. He checked the lock on the window.

After putting away his clean laundry, he laid fully clothed on his bed. Eli's mind raced with plans of leaving town. He feared the embarrassment of being discovered, the arrest, the trial, and finally prison. He knew that lawmen never fared well in jail. Eventually, he reasoned, it will all go away, he kept telling himself over and over again. Exhausted, he fell asleep.

*The German soldier's contorted face looked at him with frightened eyes as the man rose above Eli. The soldier lingered over the crest of the trench. With his bayonet fixed to his rifle, Eli stabbed fanatically at the man who did nothing to ward off each successive thrust. The man yelled, yet his cry was inaudible.*

Eli screamed. His eyes looked feverishly around his apartment, expecting something. He put a hand to his forehead and felt the sweat of panic. He moved to the side of the bed and put both feet firmly on the floor. Eli cradled his head in his hands for a while before getting up to fetch his bottle of whiskey.

On the way to his dresser, he noted the empty wastepaper basket. He thought about the crumpled sheet of paper he used to count the money.

---

## 23

Vincent Spencer was forming each of his papers into a tight roll when the door to the rear loading area opened. Looking up, he said, "Good evening, Mrs. Perkins."

"Good evening to you, too, Vincent. You're here early."

"Our teacher wasn't feeling so good."

"Nothing serious, I hope?" she asked pryingly.

Vincent shook his head. "I don't think so."

"Hmm," Olive Perkins uttered softly.

While she appeared to ponder the answer, Vincent used the lull to speak up. "Mrs. Perkins, how did you become a reporter?"

Olive Perkins whole demeanor brightened. "Well, Vincent, one does not merely become a reporter. One must study and read a lot. It takes years."

"I do a lot of reading."

She drew closer. "I'm sure you do, but it's important to know the psychology of the work, like why did the character in the story do something."

Vincent scrunched up his face. "Psy—"

"Psychology. It is the understanding of the mind and mental responses to situations. You need to go to school to learn that."

"And that's all you need to know to become a reporter?"

She smiled. "Oh, there's a lot more, but what's really important is having a nose for news."

"I think I have that," Vincent said enthusiastically.

"Your curiosity about the news tells me that, but you need to do your research. You know, you can't believe everything you read about or the things someone tells you."

"What do you mean by that, Mrs. Perkins?"

Olive tilted her head back in thought. "I mean, that some things are real by themselves, like the sun or the planets. A reporter looks for the facts because some people lie and tell you only what they want you to know. It's up to the reporter to seek out the truth."

"It sounds like a lot of work."

Olive nodded. "It is, and those papers aren't going to deliver themselves, Vincent."

"Yes, Mrs. Perkins, I'm almost done."

Olive Perkins started to leave but hesitated. She turned back; she eyed Vincent. "I'll tell you what," Olive began. "You can be my cub reporter."

"What's a cub reporter?"

"Someone who is just starting to learn how to be a reporter—a novice."

"What do I have to do?"

"Just what I said, 'seek out the truth' by keeping your eyes and ears open."

"I can do that," Vincent said willingly.

"Just a minute," Olive said and took off.

When she returned, she handed Vincent a small notebook.

Accepting it, he asked, "What do I do with this?"

"That is the most important tool a reporter can have. When you see something that is newsworthy, you jot down all the facts—who, what, when, where, why, and how."

"Who, what, when—"

Olive snatched back the notebook. "Here, let me write that down."

After passing it back to Vincent, she said, "Now, if you should see anything that is notable—jot it down and follow the six rules of the story." She handed him her pencil.

"Will do, Mrs. Perkins," he said eagerly and tucked the pencil behind his ear.

"There you go now. You look like a real reporter."

Vincent smiled proudly.

WITH ABUNDANT ENTHUSIASM, Vincent delivered his papers at the same time, attentive for anything newsworthy.

Unlike his usual quick drop off of the evening's newspaper, Vincent lingered in Miller's Grocery Store near the counter in the hope of gleaning tidbits of information from other patrons. When Mable Miller leaned over the counter to question him if he needed anything, he said, "No, Mrs. Miller, I was only looking." Leaving redfaced, he was sure his nosiness was conspicuous and vowed to himself to be less obvious in the future.

The barbershop was always a breeding ground for disjointed chatter and masculine endeavors. Vincent felt if he were to hear any news, it would be there.

"Maître Fudge, at last, ze paper."

Vincent felt at ease at hearing Louis Girard's customary greeting. "Hello, Mr. Girard. I'm actually early today."

Louis Girard looked up at the clock. "You 'av quit ze school?"

Vincent laughed. "No, sir. Our teacher wasn't feeling well today."

"Oui, Maître Fudge, stay in ze school, or else, you will end up like me." He ended his cautionary anecdote with an uncontrolled laugh that became contagious among the other patrons.

As the gaiety abated, Vincent found an empty chair. He picked up a magazine and feigned interest. While staring blankly at the pages, he secretively listened to the conversation.

After Vincent heard the political complaints, milk price, and the drought out West, he felt his deception yielded nothing of importance. Offering a goodbye, he left the shop, delivered the last of his papers, and went home.

Vincent found his mom in the kitchen, preparing supper. "How was your day?" she asked.

He was about to tell her about his new job but chose to keep that a secret. "Fine," he said and dashed upstairs to his room. When he reached the top landing, he glanced across the hallway into Lucy Lareau's room. Her door was slightly ajar. Although his glimpse was brief, he thought he saw stacks of money piled on her dresser. Vincent quickly went into his room and closed the door. Before he could stoop down to look through his keyhole, he heard the shutting of Lucy Lareau's door.

## 24

---

Helen Spencer wore a long black dress accented with a border of white ruffle at the side, capped sleeves, and a rounded neckline. Lucy Lareau, clothed in a mid-length velvet wine-red, short sleeve evening cocktail dress, adjusted her midriff. They traded self-assured glances with each other as they walked into the village hall. "I feel the burn of a lot of eyes on us right now," Lucy said with a mischievous grin.

"I feel very confident in this dress of yours," Helen said under her breath. "Thanks for letting me wear it, but I think it may be a bit much for Chandlers Bend."

"Let 'em talk."

They selected a rear table. Helen sat down, but Lucy remained standing. "I'm going to powder my nose," Lucy said. "And when I come back, I'll get a couple of glasses of punch."

While Lucy was gone, Helen played with her purse and uncomfortably scanned the gathering of attendees. She didn't look directly at them, only through them.

"Is this seat taken?" Eli asked.

Startled, Helen looked at him. "I'm sorry, I must have been

daydreaming," she said apologetically. She eyed him. "I see you aren't wearing your gun, but that tie of yours is something I haven't seen before."

Eli smiled. He held a paper bag. By its shape, it contained a bottle of something. He placed it along the wall near their table, adjusted the knot on his tie, sat down, and pulled the chair closer to the table. "Henry Blake is filling in for me tonight. Seeing I'm off duty, I figured I'd dress up."

He looked around. "I thought Lucy was going to be here?"

"She just went to the lady's room. I'm surprised you didn't see her when you walked in."

"I came through the side entrance."

Eli leaned back in his chair. "Seems like a lot of people are taking an interest in us."

"You shouldn't be surprised. After all, you are a celebrity," said Helen lightheartedly.

"I don't think that's necessarily the explanation. Other than in my official capacity as the town constable, I don't come to these shindigs. And sitting with a beautiful woman makes it more of a reason for some people to gawk and talk."

Helen smiled. "Thanks, Eli, but I know why *you* are here."

He leaned toward her. "I know, but you *are* a beautiful woman."

"Enough of that kind of talk. You're making me blush."

Eli was about to say something when he caught sight of Lucy. He rose from his chair. "My, you look stunning." He reached out to grasp her hand.

"Thanks, Eli. What a pleasant surprise," Lucy chirped, put down her drinks and took his hand before sitting next to him.

Helen gave Lucy an impish wink.

"I don't think I've ever seen such a ... um, fashionable looking dress before," Eli said as he continued to admire her.

"You should have been here when we entered the hall," Helen said. "I swear you could hear jaws dropping."

They all laughed.

"Well, maybe they aren't accustomed at seeing beautiful women," said Eli.

Helen blushed, turned away, and looked at the exit.

"Eli," Lucy began, "I heard on the radio that there was a big shoot out yesterday in New York City. Did you hear anything about that?"

"Yep. A policeman was killed."

"I heard it was awful," Helen said. "Some young thugs shot him three times. And they hurt bystanders, too—including an infant. Can you imagine that ... hurting an innocent child?"

Eli shook his head. "The newspaper account said at least twenty-five shots were fired. It's a miracle no one else died."

A somber mood descended upon the trio.

"Hey, I shouldn't have even brought up the subject. We're here to have fun," Lucy said. "I think we had enough excitement in our own town, let alone jabbering about New York."

The band started to adjust their instruments.

"Well, I guess the music is about to begin. Lucy, may I have the honor of the first dance?" asked Eli extending his hand.

The band opened with their rendition of *Temptation* as Eli and Lucy made their way onto the dance floor. Clasping each other in an embrace, they moved gently to the rhythm. Lucy rested her head on Eli's shoulder.

"You know," she began, "this is the song from the movie *Going Hollywood,* with Bing Crosby."

Eli shrugged, drew back, and looked at her briefly. "I really don't follow the latest songs."

Lucy drew him back toward her. "Well, it's not the latest song, but It's playing at the Granada Theater. I seem to recall that you offered to take me to the movies."

"You're right, I did, but I'm pretty sure I was talking about a Tarzan movie at the time."

"Why that movie? Was it the nudity?" Lucy said mockingly.

Eli moved away slightly and laughed. "You're spoiling the mood," he joked. "I don't know much about the latest music, but I think this is supposed to be a romantic song."

Lucy looked into his blue eyes, and her feigned annoyance melted. Again she drew him closer and once more rested her head on his shoulder. They finished the rest of the dance in quiet contentment.

As Eli and Lucy returned to their table, they found Dr. Brewer keeping company with Helen. "This is a pleasant surprise," said Eli.

Doc rose as they took their seats. "I was invited by my assistant." He looked at Lucy and gave her a nod. After resuming his place, he said, "She convinced me that I should get out more often. I would have been here earlier, but I had to deal with the Johnson kid. He has a bad case of the croup. So, here I am." He spread his arms in submission.

Eli got up. "Hey, Doc. Why don't you give me a hand while I get us some drinks."

"Sure thing. Let's go."

Neither of the women spoke until the men were out of hearing distance.

Lucy was the first to say anything. "I hope you don't mind, Helen, that I invited Doc?"

"Not really. I'm just a little uncomfortable. You know, this dress, the town's people staring and all that."

"Do you know what fate is, Helen?"

"I think I do. Something that is bound to happen—like death."

Lucy laughed. "Well, let's not think along those lines. No, I'm talking about romance. Look at it this way. I come into this jerk-water town and end up working for a doctor and bunking at your place. My boyfriend turns out to be a two-timing louse, and I'm with you right now and two sheiks on a date—that's fate, sister."

"Now what?"

"Helen, you're not a Dumb Dora. Right now, you gotta play the game. Doc's interested. I can tell by the way he looks at you."

Helen's eyes grew wistful. "It's been a long time since I properly dated a man. I don't know what to do."

"Hell, you don't have to do a thing. Just listen and show some interest. Let Doc make the first move. After that, it's as easy as falling off a log."

Eli and Doc returned with drinks in their hands. After setting them down, Eli retrieved his private stock and topped off each glass. He held up his glass. "To tonight," he toasted.

All the glasses clicked, and everyone took a ceremonial sip before joining the other revelers on the dancefloor.

## 25

Except for the rhythmic tick-tocking of the clock, the house was still. Vincent rested on his bed and stared at the ceiling. His mind drifted from Lucy's alluring image lying in bed to the pile of money on her dresser. One sparked adolescent fantasy—the other boyish curiosity.

Vincent rose from his bed and guided his feet into his frayed slippers. He grabbed his flashlight off the nightstand. With its light flaying at the creaking floor, he followed its beam. There was a chill in the air, yet his hands were moist. While moving into the hallway, his door protested with a squeal, which he was certain never objected to before this time. He grimaced. Vincent paused while his ears strained for other hints that his nocturnal stroll aroused anyone's attention. He knew he was alone in the house, yet he wasn't sure when his mother and Lucy Lareau would return. Feeling confident he was alone, he quickened his pace.

When Vincent entered Lucy's room, he inhaled the scent of her perfume. Something was compelling about its fragrance. His flashlight scanned the bed. Some panties, a slip, and a blue cotton dress littered its surface. He turned toward the dresser and was startled by his reflection. His mouth was dry. Starting with the top, he worked his way down, methodically opening each drawer. In his examination, he was careful not to disturb the contents. He wasn't sure what he might find. Motivated by his fleeting glimpse of the stack of money, Vincent thought only of the promised by-line and fame.

Vincent turned once more toward the bed. He saw a brown and tan striped tweed suitcase wedged between the wall and Lucy's bed closer to the window. Placing the flashlight on the window ledge, he gripped the leather handle and pulled it onto the bed. His hands trembled as he tried the slide catches—they did not budge. Another attempt proved unsuccessful, and Vincent considered using something to work the lock. The bulb on his light began to flicker and dim. With haste, he slid the suitcase back.

He removed the flashlight from the windowsill and shook it to restore its amber glow. Turning to leave, his right hand caught the vase of lilacs perched on the ledge. The feeble beam of light raced across the room as he dropped the flashlight to seize the container. Water and flowers spilled helter-skelter onto the floor. Only inches from certain destruction, Vincent snatched the vase in midflight.

Now lying prone on a wet floor, his pajamas partially soaked, his heart pounded. Vincent began to consider the predicament he faced. Instinctively he gathered the lilacs and placed them back into the now, mostly, waterless container. Vincent undid his nightshirt and used it to sop up some of the water. He thought he heard a car door slam. Now in full panic, Vincent raced out of the room to fetch a towel. Blindly running downstairs, he felt his ears burning.

He detected the distant discordant rumble of a car's engine.

Vincent grabbed a towel off the bathroom rack and charged back to Lucy Lareau's room. While wiping up the mess, he detected that water had spilled onto the rug in front of the dresser. He compressed the spot between one of the dryer ends of the towel. The glow from the flashlight began to waver again. He picked it up and struck it against his palm to revive it. He aimed it at the flowers.

*They need water.*

He raced down to the bathroom and filled a large glass with water. Rushing up the stairs, droplets of water fell on the bare steps.

With diligence, Vincent inspected the room, his panic-stricken heart slowly recovering from its distress. He eyed the vase and its blossom arrangement, unsure of their original placement. His hands patted the flowers like someone trying to relieve a loved one of pain then left.

Despite the partially opened doors of the village hall, a stratum of cigarette smoke hung lazily over the partygoers. Exhausted by the constant stream of spirited music, the mood was more restrained as each couple leaned on each other in starry-eyed support.

"I could use some fresh air," Doc said openly.

"That's not a bad idea," Eli agreed.

Lucy and Helen glanced at each other.

"Whaddaya have in mind?" Lucy asked cagily.

"Well, it's a beautiful evening. How about a ride out to Chinamans Bluff?" suggested Doc.

"It's rather dark out, and I don't think that sliver of a moon is going to brighten our path much," said Helen.

"I have a flashlight with fresh batteries. I'm guessing that Eli carries one, too," Doc said, looking at him.

"You got that right. A flashlight is part of every constable's toolkit."

With their tipsiness showing, once more, the girls exchanged glances accented with girlish laughter.

Their exit from the town hall was not without notice.

As they moved into the evening's rejuvenating air, Lucy pulled Eli close and whispered, "This will give 'em something to talk about."

Eli responded by hugging her waist as they walked toward his car.

Doc, close behind with Helen, said, "We're not going to all fit in either of our cars, so I guess we'll travel separately."

"You can if you want to, but I do have the rumble seat," Eli said.

Lucy broke free from Eli. She ran ahead to his car. With arms spread wide open, Lucy held a corner of her shawl in each hand and twirled in place. She looked as if she might fly. She cried out, "Let me ride in the rumble seat."

"If you want, but your gonna change your mind once we get going," Eli said with a smile.

"If that happens, I guess you'll have to warm me up, Eli," she teased. She hiked up her dress and exposed her shapely legs. "C'mon, Eli, give a girl a hand." Lucy offered her free hand to Eli. "Attaboy! Alley Oop, my strong caveman."

Helen laughed and looked at Dr. Brewer. "I can't say when I had this much fun, but I wouldn't mind riding along with Lucy. You'll have to warm me up, too, once we get to Chinamans Bluff," she said coyly.

Doc smiled and took Helen's hand as he helped her into the rear seat. "It'll be my pleasure."

Eli and Dr. Brewer heard the trailing screams and laughter from the back seat at the very onset of their ride.

When they arrived at the base of Chinamans Bluff, both girls enthusiastically embraced their dates for warmth. "What a ride!" Lucy shouted.

Eli grabbed a newspaper from under his front seat.

"Whaddaya going to do Eli, read while I freeze to death?" Lucy said, her teeth chattering melodramatically.

"I need this to start our fire. Come on along. We'll get you warmed up in no time," Eli said, drawing Lucy closer to him.

In charge of the flashlights, Lucy and Helen laughed and pointed their beams at potential heaps of fuel. "There's a bunch," Lucy cried out.

"What do you know about firewood?" Helen countered. "You're city slicker. There's better firewood over here." She pointed her beam in the opposite direction.

There was a rush of noise deep into the treeline. 'What's that?" Lucy asked uneasily.

"Fraidy-cat," Helen jabbered. "You probably woke a deer."

"If you don't stop yelling, you two are going to wake the dead," Doc whispered.

Eli and Lucy started up the incline leading to the top of the bluff, their light darting about haphazardly. "See you at the top," he called back. Then either through purposeful deception or terrain, the darkness swallowed their beam.

When Doc and Helen reached the summit, they saw Eli skylined against the waning glow of the moon's final quarter. Leaning over a small collection of paper, grimmia dry rock moss, and twigs, Eli cupped his hand and struck a match, directing flashes of sparks onto the tiny mound of kindling. The wind quickly devoured the flare. Again he tried, only this time drawing the budding flame closer to the paper.

It began to flicker as Eli carefully added pieces of dry moss. He blew an urging breath onto the newly forming flames then coaxed more branches into its center. As the fire craved more fuel, the group fed its hunger until its warmth and size were adequate for them to relax and enjoy the evening's ambiance.

Doc sat upright and drew Helen close to him. Eli, using his coat as a blanket, offered it to Lucy. No one spoke. Dreamy-eyed, they gazed at the logs glow as tiny embers frolicked in the updraft then wavered, surrendering to the night.

## 26

Helen stood in front of the kitchen sink. She wore a kelly green flower pot print design, dressing gown. She languidly examined the rain as it pelted against the window. In the distance, trees took on an abstract form as the streamlets of rainwater embraced the glass. Far away, the rolling vibration of thunder told her it was going to be a day for melancholy and reflection. Helen, knowing its importance to relieve the thirsty land, considered the rain a blessing. She snapped out of her pensive mood when hearing a noise from behind her. She turned and saw Lucy standing in the kitchen doorway.

"Good morning, Lucy. I was about to make some coffee."

Barefooted, Lucy wore a full-length mint-green satin dressing gown with rose front panels, her long-sleeves accented with the same rose-colored cuffs. She walked toward the table and took a seat.

"I don't know about you, but my mouth is dry, and my gams ache." She crossed her legs and passed a hand through her disheveled hair. "I need a new hairstyle," she said softly.

"Milly's in Morrisville does a real nice job," Helen said while filling the coffee pot with water.

"What's wrong with the one in town?"

"Nothing, if you don't mind having your private life discussed."

"Don't you think after last night, you and I are the topics of conversation over breakfast this morning?"

"Probably," Helen countered, her answer infused with a laugh.

"And speaking about last night, I had a great time."

"Me, too," Helen chirped. Using a hand grinding coffee mill, she began to measure out the coffee grounds. "You know, Lucy, I never did anything like that before—the all-night dancing, the ride, and the bonfire. It's all new to me. The feelings I have for Doctor Brewer—they're new, too. You know, yesterday was the first time I called him George."

"I didn't tell you this, but I went with Doc to the top of Chinamans Bluff once before."

"You did?" Helen glanced at Lucy in surprise then placed the coffee pot on the stove.

"Uh-huh."

"Why?" Helen asked, her tone accusatory.

"You must have heard about that accident on the main road?"

"Uh-huh."

Lucy smiled. "Hey, relax, and let me finish before you get yourself all wrapped up in a tizzy."

Helen sat down, leaned back in her chair, and folded her arms over her chest. "Go on."

"Doc was feeling pretty bad after seeing all those people dead. He wanted to get out of town and be alone."

"If he wanted to be alone, why did you go along with him?"

"I guess I didn't say that the right way. I meant that he didn't want to be with anyone from town ... you know, someone who ... might blabber."

"Aren't you blabbering right now?" Helen said bluntly.

"I suppose, but hear me out. Anyway, I got the feeling Doc wanted someone to listen to him besides the wind."

"And what did you two talk about?"

Lucy didn't immediately reply. Her pause appeared reflective. Finally, she said, "Mostly about how lonesome he feels."

"You sure he wasn't making a play for you with that sob story?"

"I don't think so. I told Doc I had a boyfriend. Besides, he's interested in only one person in this jerk-water-town."

Helen perked-up, "Who's that?"

"C'mon, sister, after last night, I'm surprised you even have to ask that question."

Helen dropped her hands onto her lap.

"Do you think Doc was nice to you because I invited him to join us?" Lucy said with intense ardor. "I think he's in love with you, Helen. And the only reason he hasn't asked you out on a date is that he's on the shy side when it comes to women."

"Now, what?"

"You let nature take its course. I'll be willing to bet he'll be giving you a call sometime in the near future. He might be a little slow at that, but it will happen."

Helen began to smile broadly. "I think I'd like that."

"Sister, you can count on it. I may have to nudge him a bit, but it'll happen. You can take that to the bank."

The coffee started to perk.

Helen stood up and adjusted her house robe. "I was going to make some pancakes for breakfast."

"That's all right by me, but I need some of that coffee first. Oh, and I almost forgot." Lucy dug deep into her satin dressing gown and pulled out some money. "Here's fifty bucks for my rent in advance," she said, placing the bills on the table. "It looks like I'll be hanging around this town, too, for a while."

"Eli?" Helen asked, then gave her an awkward grin.

Lucy's face agreed with a smile.

"Speaking about breakfast, Vincent is usually down here by now." Helen moved toward the staircase and yelled, "Vincent! I'll be making breakfast shortly."

Helen turned back into the kitchen and went to the stove. Using a dishcloth, she grasped the coffee pot and filled Lucy's cup before filling hers. "I'll start mixing the batter, but I'll wait until Vincent gets down here before making the pancakes."

Lucy held up her steaming cup of coffee. "I got my cup of joe. That'll keep me for a while."

From upstairs came the steady thud of approaching footsteps. The reverberation ended then faded down the side hallway and toward the bathroom. After a while, Vincent appeared in the kitchen doorway. "Good morning, Mom, and good morning to you, Miss. Lareau."

Helen and Lucy returned the greeting.

Vincent went to the table and sat down.

"You're rather quiet this morning," Helen said while mixing the batter.

Vincent's demeanor sullen—he avoided eye contact. "I'm tired. I stayed up late last night reading."

"I know it was Saturday, but you shouldn't stay up so late. It's bad for your health."

"Yes, Mom."

Unusually sheepish, Vincent stared at the kitchen window.

Lucy considered his pensive behavior while she sipped her coffee.

"By the way, Vincent," Helen began, "when we came home last night, I saw a lot of water spilled on the steps."

Vincent's face turned crimson. "Ah, ... I ... went downstairs to get some water to drink in my bedroom. I must have spilled some. That's all, Mom." He played nervously with his utensils.

"Well, be more careful next time. Someone could have slipped on those wet stairs."

"Yes, Mom."

"What does a young man do when it rains on a Sunday?" Lucy asked.

Vincent looked briefly at Lucy, then once more studied the window. "Ah, ... study or read."

"You're not acting your normal self, Vincent," Helen said as she poured the pancake batter. The skillet sizzled and popped, sending droplets of grease beyond the pan. "Is there something that you're not telling me about last night?"

"No, nothing happened, Mom. Honestly, I just stayed up late ... that's all."

"Well, I hope you're not too tired to clean up the kitchen after we have our breakfast?"

"No, Mom. I'm fine. I thought I'd go to Suzy's house and help her with her homework after I finished with my chores."

Lucy smiled. "So, Vincent, you got yourself a girlfriend?"

He shrugged. "Not really, I just like to help her. We're only friends."

"A handsome boy like you, and you don't have a girlfriend?"

"My Vincent's too busy to have a girlfriend right now," Helen interrupted. "Besides, he going to college as soon as he gets out of high school."

"Is that right?" Lucy asked.

"Uh-huh," Vincent said. "I want to be a newspaper reporter."

"Wow, that's a pretty exciting job, covering bank robberies, murders, and government corruption," Lucy said, then paused. "And a dangerous one at that, too."

Helen's mood was sullen as she placed a pancake on her son's plate.

Vincent's manner brightened as he turned to look at Lucy. "I can hardly wait," he said with fresh-faced sincerity before taking the first bite of his breakfast.

## 27

The turbulent weather moved slowly east, leaving Chandlers Bend soggy and overcast. Like most rainy Sundays, families stayed close to home, listened to the radio, read the newspaper, or played parlor games to while away the hours. Those with hobbies pursued them, those who gossiped across fences did so over telephone lines, and those who drank did so in sullen solitude.

As night engulfed the town, specks of light, like evening stars, began to populate the houses along the streets. Some quickly smothered by drawn shades or curtains tempering their radiance until only a muted glow spilled out of their loose borders. Behind the pulled window coverings, the people prepared themselves for sleep.

SUNDAY WAS the only day Helen had for herself. Feeling peaceful under her quilt she made several years ago, she reflected on her life. Before the dance, her expectations ended with Vincent's graduation. She could not envision anything beyond that. Now, with the promise of a new life, Helen fantasized about the prospect of being a doctor's wife. These were wild thoughts. They were without any basis except the wishful speculation of a widow who wanted the best for her son. *Am I in love? I think I am, but is Doc in love with me? Doctor George Brewer and Mrs. Helen Brewer—George and Helen, it has a nice ring—I like it.* From down the hall, Helen heard a banging noise.

LUCY LAREAU CLOSED the door to her closet and moved to the front of her dresser. Wearing only a pale gold slip, she studied herself in the mirror. *I do need a hairdo.* She turned and glanced at her profile, pulled in her stomach, and stuck out her chest. Sliding the spaghetti-straps off her shoulders, she let the slip drop down to her waist. Clutching the fabric around her waistline, she turned several times, each time paying attention to the droopiness of her breasts. *I'm not getting any younger.* Lucy returned the straps of her slip onto her shoulders. She twisted to one side and looked at her rear end before going to lay down. The bed's springs squealed.

THE RATTLE of squeaking bedsprings from Lucy's room conjured up an image in Vincent's mind of her lying supine on her bed. He remembered how the silken material of her slip clung to her body. He also recalled her unabashed smile at his embarrassment when he entered her room. He was sure she liked him. *If I was only a little bit older.* The sudden wail of the approaching evening train tore him from his fantasy, and he thought about the day he would take the train to Chicago and start his new life as a reporter. *I will graduate this year and start a new life.*

ELI STIRRED in bed as he heard the train rumble through town. He was in an alcohol-induced semi-slumber. His mouth dry, he smacked his lips. Tormented by his misdeed, Eli found sleep an unwilling companion. He reached for a bottle on his nightstand and took a long swig of whiskey. Like his conscience, it burned. The thought of Lucy also glowed in his heart. It was a different burn, and she was different. He acted differently around her, and her spontaneity altered the way he felt about himself. He doubted if she could understand the pain a soldier carries with him after the war is over. Now, he had added to that agony by pocketing money that wasn't his. He had become a bank robber by default. He had opened a bottle that could no longer be re-corked. The clatter from the retreating train lessened, and he rolled over onto his side.

DOCTOR BREWER WAITED at the train crossing as freight cars sped through town. He was returning from a late-night call outside of town. His thoughts were not on the colicky baby, he just left into the care of its mother, but on the people of Chandlers Bend. Years ago, he committed himself to help the sick, and he knew it was something he could never abandon. The Caboose passed with its red light vanishing into the night. Now he deliberated about his own needs. He felt something was missing—someone to share his life. As he crossed the tracks, he considered life with Helen. *Is she the one?* He often thought of her but was too shy. If it wasn't for Lucy's involvement as Cupid, would he have ever asked her out on a date? *She's refined and would make a wonderful wife. After the Saturday night dance, people are already making wedding plans for us.* Dr. George Brewer smiled at the thought.

---

## 28

Like most Mondays, business was brisk in the Chandler General Store. John Chandler was waiting on a couple of dairy farmers. Susanna Chandler stood in the back of the store near a collection of bolts of fabric. She had just finished with a customer when Caroline approached the counter. Susanna looked up. "Good morning, Caroline. How are you doing this fine day?"

"Fine. After that storm, it's nice to see the sun again."

"I didn't see you at the dance on Saturday," said Susanna looking at Caroline with inquiring eyes. "Were you sick?"

"No, I just didn't feel up to it."

"Well," Susanna began with delight, "you missed something, indeed. You know that vamp Lucy?"

"Yes, what about her?" Caroline enquired hungerly.

"She was at the dance with Eli."

"Hmm," Caroline mused.

"And that's not all," Susanna teased.

"What do you mean?"

"Well, she was sitting at the same table with Doctor Brewer, who, I may add, was in the company of Helen Spencer."

"You don't say."

"I do say, and they all left early *and together*."

"My ... my," Caroline said. "Doctor Brewer seldom goes to that dance."

"Exactly," When Lucy Lareau came into town, Beatrice Girard told me Lucy was going to be trouble."

"What do you think is going on?" Caroline asked.

"From what I hear, she came from Chicago. I'm guessing she brought some of those big-city ideas with her. I tell you, she's corrupting Doc, Eli, and Helen, too."

The bell over the door chimed as Ida Moore entered the store. She walked directly to the rear of the store. "Susanna ... Caroline, how are you doing today?" Ida asked.

"Fine," Susanna replied indifferently. "What can I do for you today?"

"I need a new scrub brush. The old one lost too many of its bristles."

When Susanna left, Caroline asked, "Been working hard, Ida?"

"Yeah, ever since that new gal, Lucy Lareau, began working for Doc, I got more work to do. She's helping him *organize,* and I think she's filling him full of new decorating ideas."

"Here's your brush, Ida," Susanna said, handing it to her.

"Thanks. Put it on Doc's account. By the way, are you still going to head this year's Fourth of July Committee?"

"Until I die," Susanna said with her chin held high.

"The reason I asked is that Lucy Lareau is complaining that there's nothing to do in our town. I'm thinking if she's got some other project to work on, besides looking for work for me to do ... ya know ... maybe she'd involve me less in her stuff. Besides, she does appear to have a gift for sprucing things up."

Susanna smiled. "I'll tell you what, you tell her that those office supplies she ordered from Milwaukee are in, and she should come and pick them up."

"Okay, but what if she tells me to do it?"

"You tell her that you were going to take it with you now, but I told you that she should come herself ... to make sure I ordered the right stuff."

A smile formed on Ida's face. "Okay, I will, and thanks."

As Ida made her way back to Doctor Brewer's office, she turned and saw the morning train slowly come to a stop in front of the Chandlers Bend station. The train infrequently stopped, so it was noteworthy for her to stare. Two men, dressed in suits with vests, one wore a fedora while the other an old style bowler hat, moved with purpose toward the Bluff Side Hotel. Each man carried a brown leather travel bag. Other than the infrequent halt and travelers debarking, she gave it no more attention and continued toward the office.

BEATRICE GIARD, already alerted by the idling train engine's racket, was at her post ready to accept guests to her hotel. "Good morning, gentlemen," she greeted warmly.

The man with the bowler hat replied, "Good morning, ma'am."

"Will you two gentlemen be catching tomorrow's train to St. Paul?

They moved closer to the counter and deposited their bags on the wood floor. "No, ma'am. We'll be catching tomorrow's train back to Milwaukee," said the man with the fedora.

"Oh? So, you have some business to take care of in Chandlers Bend?"

The man with the bowler hat reached into his coat pocket and pulled out a gold badge, and flashed it at Beatrice. It said, Pinkerton National Detective Agent. "I'm Agent Matt Knowles, and this is my partner, Agent Jack Todd. We are working for the Milwaukee Road and investigating a murder during a labor strike."

"Oh," Beatrice gasped.

"We believe our suspect may have arrived in your town," Agent Knowles said.

"What makes you say that?"

"The Pinkerton Agency has its ways, ma'am," Agent Todd replied smugly.

Agent Knowles cleared his throat. "Ma'am—"

"It's Mrs. Girard."

Agent Knowles appeared apologetic. "Mrs. Girard … has there been any new visitors that have moved into town … say, within the last year or so?"

Beatrice nodded. "As a matter of fact, there was a woman, her name—"

"No, Mrs. Girard, we're looking for a man."

## 29

B eatrice's smile withered. "Do you know the man's name?" she asked, trying to hide her unease.

"No. Although, we do have a picture of him," Agent Todd said while reaching for his travel case. He pulled out a folder, removed a large photograph, and placed it on the counter. Agent Todd pointed to a short, rotund man, positioned deep within a melee of strikers. "This is the man we are looking for."

Beatrice gazed in disbelief at the picture. Her throat became dry as she pondered the photograph. The blurred image of the man resembled her own Louis. She shook her head. "No. It doesn't look like anyone I ever saw," she said unemotionally.

Agent Todd removed the picture from the counter. "I know it's not the sharpest picture, but we were hoping there was a resemblance to someone you might have seen pass through this town."

"If you plan on staying overnight, this is the only hotel in town."

"Yes, of course," Agent Knowles said. "We'll take two rooms."

Beatrice slid the register on the counter while trying to restrain her trembling hand. "Please sign in, and that'll be one dollar each, gentlemen." She dropped both of her hands out of sight behind the countertop.

Once they left for their rooms, Beatrice, with a quaking hand, jotted down a note and sealed it in an envelope. She walked outside and frantically searched the streets. She spotted Eddie Miller. "Eddie, come here," she shouted, her throat dry with worry.

Wide-eyed, he asked, "What do you want, Mrs. Girard?"

"Eddie, take this note to Mr. Girard right now." She handed him the envelope and a quarter.

Eddie, with his palm wide open, gazed at the money.

"Eddie, you have to go *now*."

He tightened his grip on the coin, looked at Beatrice briefly with questioning eyes before taking off to the barbershop.

When Beatrice returned to her desk, she found both agents, appearing impatient, waiting for her.

"Mrs. Girard, would you direct us to your local sheriff's office?" asked Agent Knowles as he held a folder in his hand.

Beatrice glanced uneasily at the folder. "Eli Buchanan is the town's constable. His office and jail are at the end of Bluff Street, just two blocks off Main Street." She pointed in the general direction.

Both agents tipped their hats and left.

Beatrice immediately fumbled for the wall phone and took it off its cradle. She dialed the operator. "Hello, Martha. Connect me with Eli's office."

"Is there anything wrong, Beatrice?"

"No!" she snapped. "Just connect me with Eli."

The phone rang several times before being answered. "Jail, Eli Buchanan here."

The volume appeared muffled, and Beatrice knew that Martha was still on the line. "Eli, this is Beatrice."

"What can I do for you?"

She swallowed hard. "There's a couple of Pinkerton Agents heading your way. They are looking for someone who got into trouble in Milwaukee." Her voice wavered. "They have a picture of the man. I said I didn't recognize him."

There was a long pause. "Okay ... I appreciate the call. Is that it?"

"Yes, that's all. Goodbye, Eli."

ELI HUNG up the phone and thought Beatrice's call odd. He sensed ambivalence in her tone. It was an intuitive feeling. His opinion of the Pinkertons was another matter. He remembered stories his uncle told him about the Pinkertons and how ruthless they were in breaking up strikes. That image of club-wielding goons inhabited his mind.

The thud of heavy footsteps on the wood walkway leading to the jail heralded his visitors' approach. After a polite knock, without a rejoinder to enter, the door swung open. Eli rose from his chair.

"Eli Buchanan?" the man with the bowler hat asked.

"Yep. And you are?"

"Agent Matt Knowles, and this is Agent Jack Todd." Both men extended their hands in greeting. "We are with the Pinkerton Detective Agency." Only Agent Knowles displayed his badge after the friendly salutation.

Agent Knowles pocketed his badge and looked around the small office. "You have a nice cozy office, Mr. Buchanan."

"Thanks, but I'm guessin' you didn't come here to discuss my workplace."

Without waiting for an invitation, both agents sat down in the only two available wood chairs. Eli saw them take an interest in the jail cells beyond the opened door on the back of the room. He closed the door. "We don't have any prisoners back there," Eli said before returning to his seat behind the desk.

"When we were assigned to this case and found out we were going to Chandlers Bend, I immediately remembered hearing about that bank robbery you had a while back. I honestly don't recall the name of the lawman who foiled the robbery. I'm guessing it was you?" Agent Knowles asked.

"Yeah," Eli replied indifferently.

"That was some robbery. Few end up as well as that," Agent Todd said.

"It didn't end well for the robbers," Eli retorted sharply.

There was an uncomfortable silence before Agent Knowles said, "Well, for the business at hand."

Agent Todd opened a folder, pulled out a photograph, and placed it on the desk. "We are presently employed by the Milwaukee Road." He pointed at the picture. "This man is a suspect in the murder of a railroad worker, and we have a hunch that he may have come to Chandlers Bend."

Eli picked up the print and looked more closely at the man in question. "It's kind of blurry," he said.

"It was snapped by a newspaper photographer during a small riot at the stockyards. He was standing on a small platform that got jostled during the melee. The actual shooting didn't occur until just after the picture was taken," Agent Knowles said while leaning closer to the desk.

Eli placed the picture back onto the desk. "What makes you think he is the man who did the killing?"

"After the shooting, several witnesses came forward and suggested that a man fitting his description was guilty of the murder," Agent Todd said.

"So, it's hearsay evidence." Eli quipped.

"Mr. Buchanan, the Pinkertons don't deal in rumor. Our witnesses are above reproach," Agent Knowles replied tersely.

"May I ask, who are the witnesses?"

Agent Knowles snapped back. "Solid citizens, Mr. Buchanan ... a railroad engineer and one of our agents."

"Hmm, let me have another look."

Eli retrieved the photograph from his desk. He pulled out a large magnifying glass from his drawer and studied the image. After a period of contemplation, he said, "Nope. No one that I ever saw."

He slid it back at the agents.

## 30

Beatrice Girard met her husband at the back door of their hotel. She saw fear in his face. "I can explain everyzing—"

"Not here," Beatrice said. "Quick, get into our apartment," she ordered. Without a word, Louis turned and headed down the corridor with Beatrice close behind.

Beatrice, panting heavily more from anxiety than the short walk, closed her door and leaned back on it to catch her breath. She examined her husband, painfully unsure what words were going to come out of his mouth.

Clearly uncomfortable, Louis moved toward the kitchen window, his shoulders hunched, he stared outside.

"Those Pinkerton men told me why they are looking for you. Now I want to hear your side," Beatrice said, her voice quaking.

After a moment of silence, Louis cleared his throat. "*Mon chere*, I am innocent. Zee police, how do you say, framed me."

"Did you kill anyone?" Beatrice asked, almost on the verge of tears.

"*Non!*" Louis said forcefully. He turned toward Beatrice and opened his arms.

Beatrice rushed forward and buried her face into Louis' chest, and wept. "What will we do?" she cried.

While holding each other in a comforting embrace, they stiffened when they heard a knock on the door.

Beatrice pulled out her handkerchief and blotted her eyes. She motioned for Louis to go into the bedroom. With a quivering voice, she called out, "Who's there?"

"It's Eli. I need to talk with you."

Still dabbing away tears, she walked to the door, paused, took a deep breath, and opened the door. "Come on in, Eli. What do you want?" she asked, her voice tense.

"You can tell Louis to come out of hiding. I saw him leaving the barbershop, and I followed him here."

"Eli, he's innocent," she bawled.

"Calm yourself, Beatrice. I'm not going to arrest him. I only want to talk to him."

Again she pulled out her kerchief, wiped away tears, went to the bedroom, and opened the door. "Louis, Eli wants to talk with you, Louis."

Louis, shamefaced, entered the kitchen. He looked at Eli, then back at Beatrice.

"Let's all sit down," said Eli motioning toward the kitchen table.

Louis and Beatrice brought their chairs close to one another. Eli took a chair, turned it around, and straddled it. He rested his arms on the back of the chair.

Eli looked directly at Louis. "A couple of Pinkerton agents just left my office. They told me that you are a suspect in a murder. What's your side of the story?"

Beatrice patted Louis on his back. "Go on, Louis, tell him."

"*Monsieur* Eli, indeed I was there," Louis began with a quaking voice. "I was with *le groupe* of *manifestants* ... er ... how you say, protestors. Someone in zee *groupe* has zee gun and shooter 'as zee *pistolet*. I *poussé* ... pushed ... zee man and zee *pistolet* it goes off."

"Do you remember who the man was?"

"*Oui*, it was ze *chef de* train ... er ... zee *garde*."

"Just as I suspected?" Eli said.

"What's that?" Beatrice asked.

"If those Pinkertons arrest Louis, he would be tried and convicted of murder."

"Oh, no!" Beatrice exclaimed.

Louis collapsed onto the back of his chair.

"Don't worry ... don't worry," Eli said and rose. "It's pretty clear to me what actually happened. One of the railroad men had a gun and fired. Rather than charging that man with the crime, they are looking for a scapegoat. The railroad doesn't want blood on its hands."

"What are we going to do?" Beatrice begged, her kerchief at the ready.

"I'm going to stick close to those men and see what else they're up to. In the meantime, Louis, don't open your shop until those agents leave for Milwaukee and stay right here in your apartment."

Louis nodded. "*Oui*," he said meekly.

AFTER LEAVING the Bluff Side Hotel, Eli began searching the streets for the Pinkerton agents. He found them sitting in front of the Chandler General Store. Both men appeared relaxed and untroubled, considering Eli's testament that the man they were looking for wasn't in Chandlers Bend. Eli thought them too calm, bearing in mind the long train ride from Milwaukee and coming up emptyhanded.

"Enjoying our spring weather, I see," Eli said as he approached the agents.

Agent Knowles drew in a long puff on his cigar before exhaling contemptuously in Eli's direction. He appeared to dismiss the salutational remark. "Mr. Buchanan, when we met in your office, I failed to tell you exactly why we believe that our suspect came to your town."

Eli leaned his shoulder against one of the stanchions that supported the overhang in front of the store. "You gonna share that with me now?" Eli asked bluntly.

"Of course ... of course, Mr. Buchanan, sorry for the omission."

Agent Knowles took a small puff on his cigar. "I found it odd that you never asked me why I ... we ... thought our suspect was living somewhere in Chandlers Bend."

Eli noted Agent Todd's smirk, then said, "I figured someone told you, and I didn't think more of it."

"Indeed, indeed, someone did tell us. That, someone, was the conductor on the very same train that brought our suspect to your town, Mr. Buchanan."

Eli straightened up. "People come and go, Mr. Knowles. I suspect that your man did the same. He came, and he went."

Agent Knowles rose and stepped toward Eli. "Maybe Mr. Buchanan, but we're going to ask around town, just in case he slipped your detection."

"Nothing skips my detection, Agent Knowles, like those .38s you're carrying under your jackets."

"What of it?" Knowles snapped.

Eli pulled back his coat and rested his hand on his revolver. "I'm going to ask you gentlemen to surrender your weapons. In this town, the carrying of any sidearm is against the law. You can have them back when you're ready to leave." Eli reached out with his left hand.

"You have no authority. We're lawmen," protested Knowles.

"No, you're not lawmen—you're strikebreakers. Now hand 'em over."

Agent Knowles and Agent Todd exchanged glances.

"Slowly, gentlemen ... hand 'em over ... grip first."

Both men glared at Eli then slowly surrendered their guns.

"We're here to investigate a murder," said Knowles as he relinquished his revolver.

"That's police work, which makes it my job, not yours." Eli eased his hand off his revolver and accepted the weapons. "I'll lock them in my safe at the jail until you're ready to leave." Pausing in front of the frowning agents, he added, "I already told you, the man you are looking for isn't here. So, I don't want you two bothering any of our residents here in Chandlers Bend. Got that?"

Neither man spoke a word, only shooting barbs of hatred with their eyes.

Eli returned the affront with a mocking salute using their weapons to intensify his dislike. Turning dismissively away, he made his way to the jail.

Eli began making his rounds after securing the guns, alerting everyone he met that Pinkerton detectives were snooping around. He wasn't specific, only indicating that they were looking for a particular labor striker, and even giving them the time of day would be ill-advised.

Eli walked into the Chandler Telegraph newspaper office to find Charlie Perkins sweeping the front office. "Done working already, Charlie?"

"No, not really." Charlie paused, gripped his broom with two hands, and leaning slightly on it. "I'm just trying to keep up with the mess. This will be one less thing I have to do when I call it a day. It's the closest thing that I can call a break from my job. What can I do for you today, Eli?"

Eli smiled and nodded. "Is Olive around?"

"Yeah. She's in the back. You know the way." Charlie released his hold on the broom and gave a quick shot with his thumb toward the office.

Olive looked up from her desk. "Hi, Eli. Is this a social call or business?"

Eli didn't reply until he sat down on the chair across from Olive's desk. "I remember you telling me about your father and how he suffered during a strike at the Milwaukee Iron Works Mill."

"Yeah," Olive said sadly. "That was nearly forty-eight years ago, and I was around six at the time. Why are you bringing that up after all these years?"

"What's your opinion of strikebreakers?"

"Eli, you seem to be knocking at my door and not tellin' me what you want. Where is this going?"

"Okay, I'll tell you. A couple of Pinkerton agents are nosing around town, and they are looking for someone they say killed a man during a strike in Milwaukee.

Olive eased back in her chair and took a deep breath. "Wow, do you know who they are looking for?"

"Maybe. The photograph is somewhat blurry, but I'd rather not say who I think it is."

"Eli, you asked me what I think about strikebreakers. I'll tell you. My father, rest his soul, was badly injured when the National Guard opened fire on the Bay View mill's strikers. They shot him in the leg, and as a result, he became crippled for the rest of his life. So, I remember the hard times my family had because of that. It was one of the reasons I chose to be a reporter. I wanted to fight for justice, even though I couldn't do that at the time. Now I can."

"I guess then you aren't too fond of the Pinkertons."

"You got that right. The Pinkertons are scum as far as I'm concerned. They call themselves detectives. I call them bastards. Does that answer your question?"

"Yep. Well, I'm guessin' they'll be coming around pretty soon and asking you some questions."

"Eli, you can rest assured that I won't be telling them a damn thing, even if the person they are looking for is my worst enemy."

## 31

The Busy Bee tavern was crowded with dairy and railroad men and a few loggers. Eli knew it was an explosive mixture. Gus Severson and his wife, Stella, were busy tending to the customers. Except for a few patrons, the majority took no notice of him when he moved to the rear of the bar, despite the fact his lawman's shield was visible. Eli found a nook against the wall and rested his right arm on the bartop. Through the thick haze of mostly cigar and pipe smoke, he examined the multitude of drinkers, looking for the most likely to start trouble.

Gus waved to Eli and moved over to where he stood. "On duty, I see," Gus yelled over the din while glancing at his badge.

"Yep, only a glass of beer tonight, Gus," Eli called back.

Gus returned and placed the drink in front of Eli. "I'm glad you're here. With this mix, somethin' bound to happen."

Eli smiled and took a sip of his beer. As he placed his glass on the bar, he saw the two Pinkertons enter. Agent Todd was holding a folder. Both men pushed their way through the crowd, and Stella met them at the bar. From his position, Eli was unable to hear their exchange. Stella placed a couple of shot glasses in front of them and filled each with whiskey. Money was exchanged, and the contents of the glasses quickly gulped. Once more, Stella filled their glasses, only this time the men nursed their drinks. Holding their glasses, they turned and leaned against the bar, apparently trying to size up the gathering.

Eli gulped the rest of his beer and moved over to the Pinkertons. Standing close to them, Eli motioned to the folder Agent Todd held. "Still looking for your man?" Eli mocked.

"Your town isn't a very sociable place," Agent Knowles said with a smirk.

"Now, why do you say that?"

"Every person we tried to talk to clam up."

"Maybe it was your smell that put them off?"

Both men stiffened and drew closer to Eli.

"Hey, I know what you goons are up to," Eli said, standing his ground. "You're looking for a fall guy for something one of your men or the people you work for did. Now I'd advise you to scram, or I'll announce that you're a pair of Pinkerton wise guys."

A few of the nearby railroad men took note of the conversation, and Agent Todd shifted uneasily in place.

"I'd suggest you finish your drinks and leave while you can still walk out of this bar," Eli said forcefully.

Agent Todd was the first to swallow his drink, followed by Agent Knowles. Both men pushed past Eli.

"The eight-ten is usually on time, so you can pick up your guns around seven tomorrow morning," Eli said, turning after them.

After they left, Eli went back to his spot, where Gus joined him. "What was that all about?"

"Nothing, just a couple of railroad cops. I suggested they leave for their own safety."

Gus gave Eli a nod. "Another beer, Eli?"

Eli was about to reply when he caught sight of a slight dust-up that looked as if it was about to spill over into a punching match. He promptly moved to the pool table. "If anyone is going to fight, take it outside."

A burly guy, dressed in a black and red checkered flannel shirt, was brandishing a cue stick by its tapered end. "No one's going to call me a cheat!" he said and began to close in on another man who had seized another cue.

With his right hand on his revolver, Eli pushed back on the chest of the flannel-shirted man. "Ease up, or you'll be spending the night in my jail."

The man did not yield

From behind, a railroad man, dressed in striped denim overalls, took a swing at Eli and clipped his head. Eli, reeling around, punched the man square in the jaw, sending him collapsing onto the floor. The man with the black and red flannel shirt pushed Eli aside and lunged after the sprawled man. Eli caught the burly man by his left arm and spun him around. The man raised his cue. Eli lifted his left arm, anticipating a blow.

Struck, Eli yelled out in pain. He recoiled from the hit and drew his gun, pointing it at the man. "One more time, and you're not even going to make it to my jail. Now put the stick down."

Eli's left arm throbbed. He knew it was broken. "I said, put that stick down!"

The man reluctantly, but forcefully, threw the cue stick onto the pool table after shouting a few obscenities.

"You're coming with me," Eli said, nudging the man with his pistol.

The man backed up, and a few of his buddies started to close in.

"Gus!" Eli called out. "See if you can get Henry Blake to come here."

While Gus called, some of the local dairymen intervened by placing themselves between Eli and a few loggers.

"C'mon, get moving," Eli ordered, prodding the man forward.

Men moved back, forming a corridor, while Eli and his prisoner exited the rear of the bar.

Eli's arm continued to ache, and he struggled to maintain his composure. "What's your name?" he asked through clenched teeth.

The man didn't reply.

"Sooner or later, you're going to have to tell me. I'll ask you again. What's your name?"

"Jorun."

"You got a last name?"

"Jorgensen."

"Well, Jorun, I'm charging you with assaulting a police officer."

Jorun stopped. He turned uneasily toward Eli. "Listen, mister. I didn't mean ta hit ya. I was goin' for that cheatin' railroad man."

"I'll just add drunk and disorderly. Keep moving. You can tell that to the judge."

Eli saw Jorun stiffen and sensed the man was about to make a break for it. "Don't even think about running."

"You're a lawman ... you ain't gonna shoot me in the back."

"You're right," Eli agreed, "I'll shoot you in the leg, and your days of logging will be over."

Nothing more was said until they entered the jail. "I gotta pee," Jorun said.

"There's a bucket in your cell. Now move against the wall and place both arms on it."

Jorun walked through the open door of the jail cell. He looked over his shoulder at Eli.

"Turn around!" Eli barked. He placed his revolver on a nearby ledge and unhooked a set of keys from the office wall. Using his good right arm, he locked the prison door. "Put 'em down. You can relax."

"I'm thirsty," Jorun said.

"I'll get you some water when I get back."

"You're not goin' to leave me alone, are ya?"

Eli stood in the doorway between his office and cell. "You'll be fine. I'd advise you to sleep it off."

He closed the door, secured the large ring of cell keys in his desk drawer, and then left, further locking the outside door. Feeling the pain in his arm intensify, Eli turned and made his way toward Doc Brewer's office.

## 32

S hirtless, except for an athletic undershirt, Eli reclined on Doctor George Brewer's examination table.

"It's broken, all right," Dr. Brewer said. "I'll reset it, but it's going to hurt like hell, Eli."

"Got anything for this pain, Doc?"

"The best," he said and pulled out a bottle of whiskey.

"My kind of medicine," Eli said as he reached for the bottle. "Do the honors for me, will ya, Doc."

Dr. Brewer uncorked the bottle and poured a measured amount of whiskey into a large glass. "Drink this," he said as he handed the glass to him. "It'll help take the edge off."

He drained the glass in two gulps and exhaled appreciatively. "Good stuff, Doc. Now do your stuff."

Doctor Brewer carefully raised Eli's arm. Resting it on a side table, he began to manipulate it.

Eli grimaced and clenched his teeth.

"Now this is going to hurt," Doc said and quickly yanked the forearm in place.

"Shit!" Eli yelled in pain.

"Relax, the worst is over."

"I could use another dose of that medicine."

"Not right now. Let me get a cast on that arm first."

Dr. Brewer went to the sink and began to prepare a batch of plaster of Paris. Returning, he wiped Eli's arm with alcohol before applying the plaster and gauze layers. When he finished, he cut off Eli's shirt's left sleeve and handed it to him. "Sorry, it was either that or you catching a cold. Now sit up."

"How long will it take to mend?" he asked as Dr. Brewer helped him get his shirt back on.

"That cast will set-up in about fifteen minutes. The arm, maybe eight or ten weeks, maybe less. It all depends on how well you take care of yourself."

"So, can I still do constable work?"

"I can tell you that you won't be able to drive a car and shoot your shotgun at the same time."

Eli laughed.

"Okay," Dr. Brewer began, "now let me put that arm in a sling. The less you move it, the better, and the quicker it will heal."

"It's still throbbing, and it's getting a little warm."

"Oh, yeah. I forgot about your medicine." Dr. Brewer reached for the bottle and poured two glasses of whiskey. "That heat is the chemical reaction from the cast. It will eventually go away. Later, you'll want to scratch that arm but can't." Smiling, he handed the glass to Eli. "One for the patient and the other for the doctor." He reached for his drink and toasted. "To your health."

Eli smiled, downed his drink, then set the empty glass aside. "Well, Doc, I guess I'll be going."

"Not so fast." Dr. Brewer walked toward a cabinet, removed a large cotton sheet, folded it into a triangle, and went back to Eli. "You'll need this sling."

With the arm sling in place, Dr. Brewer helped Eli with his jacket. "You'll have to get used to using only one sleeve for a while."

"As long as I can walk, talk, and use my gun, I'll be fine."

"As far as the pain, I'd suggest aspirin."

"What about liquid pain reducer?"

"That's up to you, but aspirin is my suggestion," Dr. Brewer said with a wry smile.

"What's the charge?" Eli said, nodding at his sling.

"Don't worry about that. You were on the job. I'll send the bill to the town clerk."

Eli reached into his pocket and pulled out a ten-dollar bill. "Here's a little something for you. Consider it a tip."

"I can't." Dr. Brewer pushed it away.

"I'll tell you what, Doc. I'm sure you got a patient that owes you some money. You can apply it to that person's bill. Okay?"

"Okay."

Eli stroked the brim of his hat in a salute. "Now, I better get back to my prisoner."

IT WAS ALMOST midnight by the time Eli entered his office. He slipped off his coat and tossed it onto a cot. Everything was just as Eli left it. Eli unlocked his desk and fetched the cell keys. When he opened the door to the backroom, he heard loud snoring and caught a whiff of vomit. He backed out into his office.

Eli pulled out a bottle of aspirin from his wall cabinet, poured himself a drink of whiskey, and sat down at his desk. After washing down the aspirin, he opened the center drawer and removed a form. He began to write the arrest report. Finished, Eli took another large mouthful of whiskey and moved to his cot. Feeling worn-out, he sat down and kicked off his boots. Eli then questioned his ability to put them on again. His arm continued to throb. He slowly rolled over onto his right side, favoring his broken arm, pulled his coat over himself, and fell fast asleep.

## 33

When the Pinkertons picked up their guns and left, Eli attempted to go back to sleep—his attempt thwarted by the clanging coming from the backroom. With stockinged feet, he shuffled his way to the noise. He recoiled at the smell and felt it had grown more intense. "What do you want?" Eli asked, fighting his impulse to throw up.

The burly Jorun Jorgensen stood clutching the cell door with both hands. "When do I get out of here?"

"When the county sheriff comes to pick you up," Eli shot back.

Eli saw the man flinch.

"You might as well relax. It's going to be a while before the sheriff or his deputy gets here. In the meantime, I'll get you a bucket of water so you can clean up that mess you made."

"What about something to eat?"

"When you get done cleaning up, I'll get you some grub. So the quicker you clean up, the quicker you'll eat. Understand?"

Jorgensen remained quiet.

Eli turned to leave.

"Okay," Jorgensen said. "I'll clean it up."

When Eli returned, he instructed Jorgensen to back away from the cell door. Using only one hand, he unlocked the cell door, slid in the bucket with water and a rag, and locked the door again. Eli started to leave.

"What happened to your arm? Jorgensen asked.

Eli turned. "Thanks to you, it's broken."

"Hey, Mister, I'm sorry. I didn't mean—"

"Tell it to the judge," he snapped and slammed the door behind him.

Eli slumped down into his desk chair and picked up the phone, and dialed the operator. "Good morning, Hulda. Please connect me with the Bluff Side Hotel."

"I heard you had a bit of a dustup at the Busy Bee last night," Hulda said.

"Yeah. Nothing too serious."

"I heard you got hurt."

"It's nothing ... just my arm. I'm in a hurry, Hulda."

"Sure thing, Eli ... I'll connect you," Hulda said with a trace of bruised feelings.

"Bluff Side Hotel," Beatrice Girard greeted soberly.

"Excuse me, Beatrice. Hulda, thank you. Goodbye." Eli caught a slight change in the quality of the line as Hulda disconnected her phone. "Beatrice, I need a favor."

"What's that, Eli?"

"I have a prisoner that needs breakfast, and I probably could use some, too. Could you get someone to bring the meals over here? I have a bad arm and probably—"

"Don't worry about a thing, Eli. If I can't find anyone, I'll bring it myself."

"Beatrice, I heard the whistle of the eight-ten. Did those Pinkertons get on it?"

"Yes."

"Good," Eli said with relief and hung up.

Eli picked up the phone again. "Hulda, connect me with the sheriff's office."

After receiving a promise that someone would come from the

county seat to pick up Jorun Jorgensen, Eli went over to his cot only to rest but quickly fell asleep.

The knocking on his door stirred Eli from his slumber. He sat up, twisted, then positioned himself at the edge of his cot. "Hi, Beatrice. Thanks for coming."

Beatrice closed the door behind her. She rested the two-tiered lunch box on Eli's desk. "You don't look so good, Eli," she said, giving him the once-over.

"I've seen better days. Thanks for bringing the food. I couldn't ask Henry Blake because he helped me out last night. Besides, I didn't want to take him away from his job at the sawmill."

"Think nothing of it," Beatrice said. "Thank you for all you did for Louis."

Eli rose and moved toward his desk. "Those Pinkertons were only looking for someone to frame for murder by one of their own. I don't think they'll be back." He lifted the lid off one of the trays and inhaled. "Smells good."

"Scrambled eggs, potatoes, ham, and fresh bread," Beatrice said proudly, then became more somber. "What about Louis?"

"What about him?"

Beatrice cupped her hands. "Does he have anything to worry about?"

"Not from me, if that's what you're asking. If the Pinkerton agents come back, you'll probably be the first to see 'em. If they do, we'll deal with it then. Now go back to your hotel and tell Louis to open his shop. I'll be seeing him later. I need a haircut and shave."

Beatrice smiled and went towards the door. She paused and turned toward Eli. "Don't worry about those lunch boxes. I'll see if I can get Eddie Miller to pick them up." She grasped the doorknob. "Thanks again, Eli," she said before leaving.

After dropping off the food container in the cell, Eli returned to his desk and began to eat his breakfast with relish even though it was with some difficulty. Finished, he leaned back in his chair, savoring the moment.

Lucy Lareau poked her head around the door.

"Hiya," she said playfully and walked in. "I heard from the Doc that you got into a bit of a problem last night." She sat down in the chair across from his desk.

"If you mean by trouble, this broken arm, yeah."

"My, my, the tough lawman got a broken wing. You feeling any pain?"

"Only since you walked in," he joked. "How come you're not more sympathetic to a suffering old man?"

"Since I work with George, and he told me it wasn't serious ... only a clean break."

"George?"

"Yeah, George," taunted Lucy. "He insists ... less formal, he says. Jealous?"

"Maybe."

"You shouldn't be. Well, it looks like nurse Lucy has got herself a patient." She smiled. "What can I do for you, sir?"

"Do you know how to drive?" Eli asked.

"Since I was twelve."

"Good. Then how about you take me to a picture show?"

"Sounds like a great idea, but are you up to it? I mean, you look like hell ... no offense."

"None taken," Eli quipped.

"George told me to come over here and make sure you're still alive. If everything is copacetic, I'll get back to my job. You should get some sleep so you can show me a good time, mister. Got that?"

"You're one hell of a nurse," he said, rising from his chair.

Lucy met Eli halfway. She accidentally bumped his cast. "Oops, I'm sorry," she said genuinely. "Let me kiss it." She leaned forward and kissed him on the lips.

"Funny way of kissing my injury."

"Don't worry. Sometimes my kisses take the long way, but they get there."

"You're right. My arm is feeling better already."

"Good. It looks like my work is done here," Lucy said. "Now get some rest if you want to have a good time tonight. Abyssinia."

Eli took Lucy's advice and went back to his cot. He was about to doze off when there was another knock on the door. Sheriff Dawson strolled in.

"You look like hell," Dawson said.

"So I've been told. What are you doing here? I thought you'd send one of your deputies to handle this."

Sheriff Dawson went to the rear of the office and opened the back door leading to the jail cells. He craned his neck around the door frame, then closed the door. Dawson cocked his head toward the back room. "Smells a bit ripe. He giving you any trouble?"

"Mostly last night ... today, not so much."

Eli moved from his cot to the chair behind his desk.

Dawson went to the opposite side and sat down. In a subdued voice, he leaned forward and said, "Sheriff O'Neal, from Dakota County, gave me a call yesterday."

Eli shifted in place. "What did he have to say?"

"He asked me a lot of questions about you."

"Like what?"

"Like what kind of guy you are ... stuff like that."

"So, what did you tell him?"

"Told him you were an honest cop." Dawson laughed. "I didn't say anything about the bootlegging days or our differences."

Eli forced a smile. "So, why was he asking you all those questions?"

Dawson straightened up and leaned back in his chair. "That girl, the one who was Caleb Johnson's girlfriend, ain't changing her story about the money. The sheriff figures there weren't a lot of places between Red Wing and Chandlers Bend to spend over five grand."

Eli's stomach ached more than his arm. "Is he accusing me of taking the dough?" Eli said, raising his voice.

Dawson shook his head. "I don't think so. I think he's under a lot of pressure. You know, the death of the bank teller in Hastings and the missing money. I just thought you'd be interested. Hey, enough talk about that. I only came here for your prisoner."

## 34

Lucy Lareau walked into Eli's office and found him resting on his cot. "I hope you got a good nap today?"

Eli swung around and stood up. "Yeah. After Sheriff Dawson picked up my prisoner, I was able to catch a few more winks." He eyed Lucy. "You're looking good."

"Thanks. You're not looking so bad yourself. I see you changed your outfit and got a haircut and shave."

"Yep. I had a hell-of-a-time getting my boots on. The shave is thanks to Louis. And I did have some trouble cleaning up with only one arm."

Lucy beamed. "That's where a nurse comes in handy."

"Maybe this broken arm is going to turn out to be a good thing."

"Who knows, but right now, we better get going if we're going to make it to the show on time," Lucy said as she held the door open. "I see your car is out front. You got enough gas in it?"

"Yep. You told me you know how to drive."

"You bet I do. Like I told you before—since I was twelve."

Eli looked at her with some misgivings. "Yeah, but when was the last time you *actually* drove a car?"

"Two years ago," Lucy said with a smile. "It's like riding a bike. You don't forget."

Eli locked his office and gave her the keys to the car. "Okay, little lady, it's all yours, but my car has a little more power than your legs."

Lucy faced Eli and raised the hem of her red dress slightly above her knees. "You sure about that?" she teased.

The smile on Lucy was tantalizing. "You're full of surprises," he said before he turned to get into the passenger side of the car.

She smoothed her dress and strolled in front of Eli's tan and black 1931 Buick Coupé, keeping eye contact with him until she jumped into the driver's seat. "Let's see," she mused openly. She glanced at Eli. "Don't look at me—you're making me nervous."

Eli shrugged. "Okay, but if you need any help—"

"I'm fine," she snapped. Lucy inserted the ignition key, turned it, pulled out the choke, put the shift in neutral, and with some difficulty reaching the floorboard, pushed the starter pedal. The engine thundered.

Eli said, "Ease up on the choke."

"I know, I know." Lucy pushed in the clutch and put the Buick into gear, then released the clutch. The car lunged forward.

"Easy … easy," Eli shouted.

Lucy straightened up in her seat and smiled. "Don't worry. Everything is under control." She tested the horn, looked at Eli, looked back toward the road, and put the car into second gear. Theirs was the only vehicle moving down Main Street as Lucy made her way toward the state highway.

Once on the road to the county seat, Eli relaxed. "By the way, what's the name of the movie?"

"*Twentieth Century*," Lucy said. "It's starring John Barrymore and Carole Lombard."

"I don't pay much attention to the movie schedules. What kind of movie is it?"

"It's a comedy. I hear it's really good. Just the thing to bring you out of your sour mood."

Eli rubbed the back of his neck. "Why did you say that? I mean, why do you think my mood is sour?"

Lucy kept her eyes on the road. She said, "You're acting like you got a burr under your saddle. You were more ... ah, good-humored earlier. I'm guessin' the arms got you down."

Eli remained silent.

"Hey, cheer up. We'll see the picture show, get a bite to eat, and maybe if you're really good, I'll take you for a ride to Chinamans Bluff."

"With this arm, I'm not too sure I can make the climb."

"Well, then, we'll find something else to do."

Eli turned to Lucy, and their eyes met. They exchanged smiles. Lucy veered off the road for a few seconds, sending dirt and gravel into the air before regaining control of the vehicle again.

"Whoa, take it easy!" Eli yelled. "Ya gotta keep it on the road if we're ever gonna make it to Chinamans Bluff alive."

ELI AND LUCY walked out from under the protective cover of the theater's marque and moved across the street. "Did you ever eat here?" Lucy asked, eyeing the bright lights and noticeable clusters of diners visible through the line of windows that faced the road.

"Sure. We don't have a lot of choices as you did in Chicago. Most of the other restaurants close early. *Nicole's Nook* stays open pretty late."

"How's the food?" she asked as Eli held the door with his free arm.

"You'll find out yourself, but I can tell you now that you won't be disappointed. Nicole's husband, John, was a cook in the navy. People in these parts say he makes the best-smoked ribs."

The restaurant appeared full of activity. A waft of seasoned air welcomed them as they pulled open the door. Nicole spotted Eli and greeted him. "Well, as I live and breathe, if it isn't Eli, the hero of Chandlers Bend. And what's with the arm? You fall out of bed?"

Eli laughed. "No. I got into a fight with one of them loggers that are doin' some clearing east of town."

Nicole eyed Lucy. "Ya gonna introduce me to your friend, or are you ashamed of me?"

"Nicole, this is Lucy Lareau," Eli said, self-consciously and gestured toward Lucy. "We just came from the show house. Do you have any of John's smoked ribs left?"

"Gettin' pretty close to the end, but we'll take care of you. John's been making extra, cuz of that new Lombard picture."

"Besides the picture show business, how you been gettin' along?" asked Eli.

"What's saving us are them truckers. God knows where they are comin' and going from, but they just keep on a-comin'. Now, let me find you two a nice spot where you can sit and enjoy some of John's ribs."

Eli and Lucy were led through the tight maze of chairs and tables. A few patrons looked up as they made their way, glancing mostly at Lucy. When they reached the far end, they slid into a narrow booth.

"Considering we ain't got much left 'cept ribs and mashed taters ... I'm guessin' that's all right with you?" Nicole asked.

Lucy nodded. "Sounds good to me."

"A couple of coffees, too," Eli shouted to Nicole as she was leaving.

"So, what did you think of the movie?" asked Lucy. "I saw you were laughing a lot, so you must have enjoyed it."

"Yeah, it was funny. You know that Carole Lombard reminds me of you in some ways."

Lucy smiled. "How so?"

Eli leaned back and studied Lucy. "In the movie anyway, she's independent and forceful."

"What do you mean by forceful?"

"Well, you appear to know what you want, and nothing is going to get in your way."

Lucy studied her hands. She looked up. "I suppose you're right," she said flippantly. "And what do you think I want?"

Eli gazed squarely into her eyes. "I'm thinking it might be me."

Lucy laughed. A flush grew on her face. "Don't be so sure of your-self, buster."

Smug in his demeanor, Eli said, "Hey, in my line of work, you get to know people."

"So, you think ya know me, hey?"

"Yep."

"And what do ya think I'm up to?"

"Having this arm in a sling puts me at a disadvantage. In my weakened condition, who knows what will happen."

Lucy smiled. "Yeah, who knows."

Both Eli and Lucy looked up when Nicole returned with their order.

"Looks delicious," Lucy said, eyeing the plate in front of her.

"Yes, it does," Eli said but remained staring at Lucy.

AFTER ARRIVING at the base of Chinamans Bluff, Eli and Lucy switched places. Lucy cuddled next to Eli.

"I have a blanket in the rumble seat," Eli said.

Lucy slipped her hand between Eli's broken arm and his chest. "No, this is fine. It's a bit chilly out."

For a moment, they sat together, each with their thoughts. Finally, Lucy said," You're right."

Eli looked at her. "About what?"

"About what I want."

"And what do you want?"

"You," Lucy said and gently kissed him.

Eli, feeling the desire, shifted and drew her closer.

Lucy breathed heavily and with open lips met his.

## 35

Vincent heard the groan of the floor, followed by the closing of Lucy's door. He looked at his clock and noted it was almost two. He listened intently. *Perhaps she is drunk?* But he only heard shuffling and the occasional closure of drawers. Next followed the squeak of mattress springs—then silence.

Now in the stillness of the night, Vincent only heard his breathing punctuated by the stimulated throbbing of his heart. Part of his anxiety, fueled by infatuation, shared space with his earlier effort at prying. In the rapture of the intrigue, he devised a plan for another attempt to explore Lucy's room. He was sure he would get another chance; it was only a matter of time.

"You look tired," Helen said as Lucy entered the kitchen. Although tired herself, awake half the night listening for Lucy's return, she was still in her flower pot print, dressing gown, too tired to change into her usual house dress.

Lucy smiled, "I am, but I feel great."

"Any reason why?" Helen asked as she laboriously whisked eggs in a crockery bowl.

Lucy twirled in place, her full-length mint-green satin dressing gown opening a bit. "I think I'm in love."

Putting down the bowl, Helen asked, "Eli?"

"Uh-huh," Lucy chirped.

Helen went to the stove and picked up the coffee pot. "Coffee?"

"You bet. I think I could use a gallon of the stuff today."

"Well, that was quick," Helen said as she filled Lucy's cup.

"Not that quick. I think I fell in love with him the day I arrived here in Chandlers Bend."

Helen filled her cup, then joined Lucy at the table. "What about Eli? How does he feel?"

With bubbling enthusiasm, Lucy said, "He was stuck on me, too —from the first day we met! Can you imagine that? The first day we met!" She grabbed her cup with both hands and blew wistfully over the steamy brew.

"I heard you come in last night ... well, actually this morning," Helen said, her weary eyes hovered over the rim of her cup while hiding her demure smile behind it.

Blushing, Lucy put down her coffee and beamed. "Right now, Eli needs me. I'm goin' to help him. So, I may be coming in late now and then, until he gets back on his feet, so to speak."

Helen nodded. "That's fine by me, just—"

Vincent, his hair neatly combed and dressed in corduroy slacks and a blue checkered flannel shirt, rounded the corner and entered the kitchen. "Good morning, Mom ... Miss Lareau."

"Good morning," Helen answered calmly. "I was about to make scrambled eggs with some fresh bread."

"I'm starving," Vincent said bashfully as he cautiously took his seat at the table.

Lucy looked at him with interest. "Good morning, Vincent."

He shifted uneasily in his chair."

"Good morning," he said silently, giving Lucy a subdued smile.

The cast-iron skillet sputtered as Helen poured the beaten eggs into the pan.

"So, how are you doing as a cub reporter? Any interesting news?" Lucy asked playfully.

Vincent shrugged. "Nothing much."

Lucy smiled. "Oh, I bet in a town this size, you could learn a lot about what's going on."

He looked at her with interest. "Like what, Miss Lareau?"

"Hmm, let's see. Ya gotta hang out in taverns. That's where people talk with greased lips."

Helen shot Lucy a look of disapproval.

"What's greased lips?" he asked.

"That's just a saying. It means that people talk more openly when they have a drink or two in them."

"Well, that's a long way off, Vincent," Helen said as she portioned out eggs onto his plate. "Now, eat your breakfast, and don't bother Miss Lareau."

"He's not bothering me. I think it's sweet that he wants to be a reporter. Ya know Vincent, people do a lot of talking in places other than gin mills."

"Like where?" he mumbled, his mouth crammed with food.

"Don't talk with your mouth full," Helen chided.

Lucy considered the question. "Like the post office, the general store ... the barbershop ... and ... ah, the gas station. The gas station is a swell spot to gather information—people are coming and going all the time, and they see stuff."

Vincent appeared mesmerized. "Wow, you know so much, Miss Lareau."

"Ya learn a lot of stuff in Chicago," she said offishly.

"Someday, I'm going to go to Chicago and learn stuff, too."

"Well, right now, finish your breakfast and get ready for school. You won't get to Chicago until after you graduate," Helen said uneasily.

"Helen," Lucy began, "I think I need some new clothes. Any chance that you could take me to Morrisville?"

For a moment, Helen stood still and appeared frozen in thought.

"Helen?" Lucy coaxed.

"Oh, I'm sorry." Helen dished out some of the eggs onto Lucy's plate. "Did you say something?" she asked coolly.

"*I said*, could you give me a ride to the county seat? I'd like to buy a couple of new dresses."

Helen indifferently scrapped the remaining eggs onto her plate. When she put the skillet into the sink, it hissed, sending a plume of steam into the air. Dreamily, she observed the mist dissolve before taking her place at the table. "When did you want to go?"

"Today's Wednesday. So, I really won't be able to go until Saturday. How does that sound?"

"Can I go, too?" Vincent asked.

Helen looked inquisitively at Lucy.

"I'd thought it would be nice if it were just the two of us," Lucy said.

Helen saw his enthusiasm fade. "You can go another time," she said. "Besides, I want you to clean out the garage."

Vincent frowned.

The sympathetic wink that Lucy gave him appeared to improve his disposition. "I better get going," he said and picked up his plate and deposited it into the sink.

Once Vincent left, Helen said, "I'm surprised he didn't put up more of a fuss. Usually, he goes on and on. A little disappointment in life is good for him—it builds character. Besides, I could use a break."

"Yeah, it'll be fun," Lucy said.

## 36

Olive Perkins, engrossed in the Chandler Telegraph's current edition, looked up when Vincent walked in. "Hi, Vincent. I think you're going to like tonight's banner headline."

Vincent put down his empty newspaper bag and approached Olive. "What is it?"

"They got the Barrow Gang!" She showed him the headline: "TEXAS OFFICERS TRAP AND KILL CLYDE BARROW AND BONNIE PARKER."

Vincent's eyes flashed. "Wow!" He reached out as Olive handed him the paper. Vincent skimmed the front page, an older picture of the two of them set within the center of the article. "I can't wait to deliver this," he said, still captivated by the news.

"Well, I suppose you better start rolling up those papers," she said, pointing to the stack on the receiving dock, "if you plan on delivering them today."

He put the paper aside. "Yes, Mrs. Perkins."

Vincent started to turn each paper into a nice tight roll.

"By the way, Vincent. How are you doing as my chief cub reporter?"

He thought about Lucy Lareau but dared not say anything. Telling Olive of his suspicions would surely bring displeasure from his mother. He remembered an admonishment his mother told him several times. *"What happens in this house stays in this house."*

"I haven't heard anything interesting," he said with downcast eyes. Then to appease Olive's curiosity, he blurted, "I overheard that Miles Gunter is planning on selling some of his dairy cows for hamburger meat. Sez he'll get more money."

Olive smiled. "I don't think he was serious about doing that. Even though milk prices are low, I think he was just saying that out of frustration with the current state of the economy. But, I'm glad you're paying attention. Just keep your eyes and ears open. We'll see if we can't get you a byline in the paper someday."

Vincent glowed with anticipation of having his name appear in the *Chandler Telegraph*. "That'll be swell," he said, rolling up each paper with renewed enthusiasm. The promise of his name appearing in the newspaper and the announcement of the Barrow Gang's killing spurred him on. Motivated, he happily left on his paper route.

On the street, he eagerly proclaimed to each customer he encountered, "Read all about it, Bonnie and Clyde, killed in a Louisiana shootout." Not aware of what happened, customers took the paper from his eager hand and promptly buried their faces into the news account. Again, Vincent wanted to yell, *Extree! Extree! Read all about it.* But it wasn't a special edition, like Chicago, but it silently played in his brain like it was. *What a day!*

Upon entering Doctor Brewer's office, he saw Lucy Lareau coming out of an adjoining room.

She smiled and put down a file folder on a nearby desk. "Why, hi, Vincent. You look pretty happy this afternoon," Lucy said as she approached him with her hand extended.

He was happy. Just seeing Lucy made him happy. Dressed in a tan and multi-colored floral print day dress with puffy sleeves, she appeared to float as she walked toward him. A gentle wisp of perfumed air surrounded her, and he eagerly inhaled. "I am happy," he said proudly. "Here's Doctor Brewer's paper. Some lawmen in

Louisiana shot and killed Bonnie and Clyde," he said boldly, almost as if he was responsible for their death.

Lucy looked at him with uncertainty. He sensed her misgivings. "Well, I mean, they won't be robbing and killing other people. That's good, isn't it?"

She nodded. "Well, yes, it is, Vincent. But, killing isn't something very pleasant to talk about." She took the paper from his hand. "Thank you."

Vincent turned, feeling a bit embarrassed, started for the door.

Lucy called out. "Vincent, I won't be having dinner with you tonight. Eli and I will be going out to eat. Your mom already knows. So, I'll see you at breakfast tomorrow."

Vincent turned and gave her a casual wave. "See you tomorrow," he murmured and exited, holding his near-empty newspaper bag.

GIRARD'S BARBERSHOP was empty of customers. Louis Girard gave Vincent a halfhearted welcome, "*Maître* Fudge, you have done your paper route? No?"

"Yes, Mr. Girard. Here's the latest news about the Barrow Gang. They were killed yesterday in a shoot-out down south."

Louis Girard reached out and took the paper from Vincent. "*Merci beaucoup,*" he said listlessly and did not attempt to engage Vincent.

Vincent, sensing his reluctance, left without saying anything other than "Goodbye."

Once home, Vincent saw that the door to Lucy's bedroom had been left open. He walked beyond the threshold and inhaled the sweet-smelling fragrance of her essence. Almost immediately, he heard his mother rummaging near the downstairs landing. Afraid she may decide to come upstairs—Vincent hurriedly ran across the hall into his room.

His heart raced out of fear of being caught poking around. He knew it was foolish to even be in Lucy's room with the possibility that his mother or even Lucy, for that matter, may find him. What would he say? What excuse could he offer? He couldn't think of an answer. But, on Saturday, when his mother and Lucy were shopping, he would have the entire house to himself. That would be his time to find out.

Vincent remembered; *Who? What? When? Where? Why? How?* He went into his dresser and pulled out the notebook Olive Perkins gave him. He looked at the list she wrote for him. *Who? That would be Lucy Lareau and maybe someone else. What? The money. When did she get it? Where did she get all that money? Why is she here in Chandlers Bend? But most importantly, how did she get that money?*

His mind reeled. *After Saturday, I will know all the answers. After Saturday, I will have my first story and byline. After Saturday, I am going to be a reporter.*

## 37

"Well, I'm surprised to see you up so early on a Saturday," Helen greeted Vincent as he entered the kitchen.

Vincent was equally surprised seeing his mother in her tan midi dress. The only time she wore that dress was when they went to church. "You're all dressed up. You look good, Mom," he said, approvingly, then surveyed the kitchen.

"Aren't you going to have breakfast before you go, Mom?

"Lucy thought we should get an early start." Helen adjusted her keyhole style short sleeve cuffs. "We're going to get something to eat in Morrisville," she said while admiring her reflection in the kitchen door window. "There's a couple of hard-boiled eggs for you in the icebox. For lunch, you can make yourself a peanut butter sandwich. Mrs. Henderson gave us some wild plum preserves. You can have that with your sandwich."

"Good morning Miss Lareau," Vincent said as she entered. He thought she looked quite striking wearing her blue and white plaid dress with a sashed belt and white bow collar.

Helen spun around and greeted Lucy. "Good morning, you look great."

"You, too, Helen. Let's get going before they run out of things to buy."

Helen laughed. "All I have to do is get the car out of the garage."

Vincent couldn't remember the last time he saw his mother this happy.

Helen waved to Vincent as she and Lucy left through the back door. Moments later, he heard the rumble of his mom's 1925 Ford Tutor Sedan. He went to the front window and saw the car fade down the street, a blur of blue smoke trailing behind.

Feeling free of time restraints, Vincent turned on the radio, tuning it to the Tarzan series. He reached into the icebox, picked out the eggs, and placed them on the table. After slicing a piece of bread, Vincent buttered it and set it alongside the eggs. He ate his food enthusiastically before washing it down with a tall glass of apple cider. Finished, he put the dirty dishes in the sink, intending to clean them after checking Lucy Lareau's room.

Without the need for secrecy or stealth, Vincent turned up the radio's volume and scrambled to the second floor. Once inside Lucy's room, he eyed the placement of everything, carefully noting their arrangement, mindful everything needed to appear undisturbed when he was through.

The bed was unmade. Lucy's full-length mint-green satin dressing gown, with rose front panels, appeared to have been thrown hastily on the foot of the bed. On top of it, paper money with a five-dollar bill embracing what appeared to be several more dollars. He was not motivated by thievery, only research for his news article. He immediately went for the suitcase he saw during his previous foray, which had been wedged between the wall and bed.

It was gone. Vincent dropped to the floor and pushed aside the hem of the duvet. He peered under the bed. Nothing, but as his mother would say, "dust bunnies."

Vincent turned toward the closet and opened the door. Dresses and other lady things were hanging from a wooden pole that stretched between the cubbyhole walls. High above the pole was the suitcase with its brown and tan striped tweed covering resting on a shelf. The leather handle faced him. Even for his above average height, it was out of reach. He looked around the room for something to stand on.

*How did Lucy get it up there? The chair near the dresser was probably used.*

Vincent wasn't sure if it could hold his weight.

Remembering the stepstool in the kitchen, he ran downstairs to fetch it. As he was about to mount it after his return, Vincent thought of a better idea.

*Perhaps the reason for its placement was because it was empty.*

He was drawn to the dresser, where he started with the top left drawer and cautiously opened it. It was crammed with panties, stockings, and slips. Leaving everything in place, he gently pushed down on the collection. He felt for any lumps that would suggest the presence of stacks of money.

Moving his attention to the drawer on the right, he became a bit more careless. The contents clinked as small bottles and other toiletries bumped one another. He winced. Again nothing. He went back to the left side and opened the bottom drawer. A small blanket filled the interior. Vincent carefully lifted a corner and pulled it back. He saw a copy of the *Chandler Telegraph* newspaper. The headline concerned the Dillinger Gang and the death of John Hamilton. He picked up the paper and became alarmed when a pistol slipped from its fold, hitting the drawer bottom with a thud.

Vincent's heart raced. He plucked the gun out of the dresser drawer. It was the first time he held a gun like this one. It wasn't at all like Eli's revolver. Keeping it in his damp hand, he appraised its weight. It was heavy. Vincent got up and grasped the weapon with both hands. He played with a lever on its side. Raising it slowly, Vincent pointed it toward the window. "Stick'em up, you dirty, double-crossing rat," he said in an unconvincing adolescent impersonation of James Cagney.

From behind, he heard the floorboard moan. Vincent immediately turned. Lucy's eyes were fixed on him and appeared to boil over in anger. Out of fear, his shaking hands tightly gripped the gun's handle.

"What are you doing in my room?" she shouted.

Vincent's brain whirled like a county fair's game of chance. Fearing the consequence of his action, his face burned with shame. His mouth, wide open, remained voiceless.

Lucy reached for the handgun and yanked it from him.

It fired.

## 38

Vincent froze. The gun leaped from his hands as the bullet struck Lucy's left breast.

She let out a feeble gasp before falling to the floor.

He wailed one long shriek of despair. Vincent's breakfast rose from his tormented stomach. He tried to force down the bitter bile that burned his throat. His efforts failed him—vomiting on the unmade bed.

Trembling, Vincent ran his finger through his hair.

*What did I do? God, what did I do?*

He began to bawl uncontrollably. His legs became rubbery. He thought they might not support him. From below, he heard a surge of footfalls.

Vincent's mother called out. "Lucy! Is something wrong?" Helen's staccato steps were interrupted by another call. "Lucy?" her voice closer. Finally, in a rush, she stood outside Lucy's room and shrieked. "What happened? My God, what did you do?"

Vincent saw his mother's eyes travel from Lucy's body, then back to him with unbelieving eyes. Vincent, sensing her anguish, dashed past and fled down the stairs. His mother's screams grew fainter the farther he ran. The family Ford stood idling in front of their house as Vincent sprinted down the street. Planless, he only wanted to escape.

*Why? Oh, Why? Why did I go into that room?*

Vincent panicked. Burning with regret and grief, he felt the full weight of his action with each hurried step. With wild determination to distance himself from his crime, Vincent ran through the village streets, then north onto the state highway. Seeking the cover of the forest, he rushed blindly into the tangled mesh of undergrowth.

Branches flayed at him as he charged through the brush. The thorns of the black locust trees pulled at his clothing and clawed at his skin. Gulping in air, Vincent began to slow down. He was soaked with sweat and splattered with dew. Without resources, except for a pocket knife, Vincent collapsed on a bed of damp oak leaves and wept.

## 39

Helen screamed, "Lucy! Lucy! Get up." Helen's hands grasped Lucy's shoulder and shook her as if trying to wake someone from a deep slumber. Terrified, she ran down the stairs, unhooked the phone from the kitchen wall, and yelled into its receiver, "Hello, hello, ... Hulda?"

"Well, hi, Helen. What—"

"This is an emergency! Get Doctor Brewer. Lucy's been shot. Hurry! And get in touch with Eli." Helen slammed down the phone, then ran back upstairs in a panic. Again, she tried to revive her.

Moments later, she heard the rush of people bounding upstairs. Eli was the first person to enter the room. Without hesitation, he dropped to his knees and, with his uninjured arm, pulled Lucy to his chest.

"Lucy? It's me," he said softly. "Can you hear me?"

Her head swayed backward. Her eyes, once so full of sparkle, had a blank stare. Lucy's mouth remained open as if fixed in a perpetual cry of shock.

Tears streamed down Eli's cheeks. He slid his arm along Lucy's back, gently cupped her head in his hand, and drew it to his chest.

"Lucy ... Lucy," Eli cried, kissing her forehead, then tenderly rocking her lifeless body in his embrace.

His breath labored, Dr. Brewer pushed his way past some of the onlookers gathered at the top of the stairs. Holding his black satchel in his hand, he immediately joined Eli. "Eli, please ... let me have a look," Dr. Brewer said as he retrieved a stethoscope from his bag.

Eli eased Lucy onto the floor but kept a hand joined to one of hers.

Dr. Brewer leaned over Lucy, pulled open the collar of her dress, and then placed the stethoscope's chestpiece bell on her left side.

A hush descended upon the room.

Following a protracted silence, Dr. Brewer closed his eyes and exhaled. With his eyes still shut, he removed the stethoscope from his ears and paused before opening them again and turning toward Eli. Doc shook his head slightly.

"I'm sorry," he whispered.

Dr. Brewer closed Lucy's eyelids and pushed up her slackened jaw. He reached over to grab the blue blanket that lay beside her draping it over her body before coaxing Eli back onto his feet. "Come on. There's nothing more I can do."

Helen, in shock, began to cry. Through a veil of tears, she looked at a dazed Eli, hoping to find support, but only saw a reflection of her despair.

"How did this happen?" Eli blubbered.

She wasn't sure herself, except Helen, knew her son was responsible. She faltered. "I ... I ... I'm sorry ... Vincent—"

"Vincent? What about him?"

Helen looked down, trying to avoid his incredulous stare.

"I don't know. We were halfway to Morrisville when Lucy ..." Helen drew her hand over her mouth and tried to stifle a sob. "When Lucy said she left her money on the bed."

Helen shifted her vacant gaze back to Eli. He nodded impatiently, his visible intolerance burning into her already aching heart. "Okay, then what happened?"

"We came back here. I waited in the car while Lucy ran inside the house. That's when I heard a loud noise. I became concerned. She wasn't coming. When I found her lying..." Helen bawled. "Vincent was standing over her body. Oh, God! Oh, God! How could this have happened?"

"He did this?" Eli asked, his voice rising in disbelief.

With tears streaming down her red cheeks, Helen nodded.

"How? Does Vincent own a gun?" Eli asked, his furious tenor lashing at her already pained heart.

"No, of course not!" Helen yelled back, quaking at the notion. The lingering stench of the room and the web of people pushing to gawk made her feel trapped.

Dr. Brewer put his hand on Helen's shoulder. "Easy, Eli, she's been through a lot already. Is there anything else, Helen?" he asked softly.

She pulled away and started for the door. "I have to find my son. He needs me."

"Helen," Doc Brewer called out before reaching her. He gently embraced her waist and began to guide her out of the room. He paused, still holding Helen, he turned to Eli. "I think you should let Sheriff Dawson handle this. In the meantime, I'll contact the county coroner."

Helen followed Doc's lead as they pushed their way past the crush of people. She hated their judgemental stares, knowing they will distort the truth into something sordid. Fleeing the nightmare, Helen heard Eli driving the curious out of the hallway as he turned to go down the staircase.

Once in the kitchen, Helen heard Dr.Brewer make his calls. Finished, he approached her as she hid her face into the hollow of her crossed arms. He patted her back. "I'm going to give you something to make you sleep."

She sprung up. "I don't want anything. I just wanna find my boy."

"Helen," he said sternly, "you're going to have to leave it up to the sheriff. You don't have a clue where he went. Come on, let's go into your parlor."

Helen looked at Doc, her eyes raw from crying. "George, what do you think they're going to do to Vincent?"

Dr. Brewer helped Helen to her feet. "He's not the kind of kid who would willfully harm anyone. I'm sure there's a good explanation for what happened."

"I'm afraid he's going to do something rash before we know the truth," Helen lamented and moved, trancelike, into her front room.

"Lay down on your sofa. I'm going to get you a glass of water." Exhausted, Helen agreed and let Doc help ease her down.

She curled herself into a fetal position.

Within a few minutes, she heard Dr. Brewer's measured steps as he returned. "Helen," he said softly.

She turned toward him and reached out listlessly to accept the sleeping pills.

"Here, this will make you sleep."

Reluctantly, she accepted and took the glass of water from his hand.

When she finished, Doc Brewer covered her with a quilt taken from the back of the sofa, then tucked it around her.

"Now you rest, I'll take care of everything," Doc said to her as she slipped into oblivion.

## 40

E li Buchanan caught a glimpse of Olive Perkins pushing her way through the crowd gathered in the village hall. Inside, there was a cacophony of noise. She approached Eli. "I just heard the news. There must be some mistake. Vincent couldn't think of willfully killing anyone."

Eli, unreceptive to Olive's remarks, cleared his throat. "I need everyone's attention!" he barked.

The rumble of conversation slowly faded but didn't cease.

"Dammit, listen up!" Eli yelled.

The room became still.

Eli scanned the assembly. "As you all must know by now, Lucy Lareau has been killed. The suspect in the slaying is Vincent Spencer."

A wave of astonishment flooded the hall.

"Hold it down and listen up."

Fighting back the tears, Eli asked, "Did anyone here see him this morning?"

Caroline Dunlop raised her hand. "I did. He was running east, toward the state highway. He was acting a little funny."

"Yeah, and I saw him hightailing it north," shouted Ted Shutter. "I was pumping gas at the time."

Eli nodded. "Okay, that's a starting point. I need volunteers to help find him. I don't want any rough stuff, either. Got that?"

Someone asked, "Does he still have the gun?"

"No," Eli said emphatically. "And speaking about guns, I don't want any weapons when we're out there. I won't tolerate any vigilante stuff. I only want to bring him in so he can tell his side of the story. Do you understand? No violence."

Whispers of disbelief fanned the gathering into full disorder.

"Calm down," Eli ordered. "Everyone here knows Vincent, and you all would have to agree that this isn't something he would do on purpose. So, if somebody here thinks we are out for his blood, they can stay in town. Now, who wants to come with me?"

A chorus of me's and I will's echoed within the hall.

Henry Blake approached and pointed to Eli's cast. "You can't drive with that."

Eli nodded. "I know. I'm looking for a driver. I guess you're it," he said with a forced smile. "I'll ride up front with you, and we can fit two more people in the rumble seat."

"Where we going?" asked Henry.

Eli called out. "Miles, come here."

Miles Gunter pushed his way through the crowd. "What d'ya want?"

The crush of town's people began to talk boisterously among themselves.

"Everyone, shut up and listen," Eli yelled. "Miles, I want you to take charge of the group leaving from town. Vincent has a head start. It shouldn't be too hard to follow his tracks in the morning dew. He's not going to go east because of the swamp. The bluffs west of the state highway are too high. So, I'm guessin' he'll stay somewhere between the state highway and the wetlands. Henry and I are going north of Chinamans Bluff, then swing south through the woods. We should be able to flush him out. And just in case Vincent does decide to make a run for the buttes, I want someone to patrol the highway. Now let's get going."

Ted Shutter offering his truck for transportation, joined the others in organizing a caravan. There was a holiday eagerness, tempered with the solemnity of a funeral that spurred everyone to action. The motorcade, wrapped in a cloud of exhaust fumes, snaked its way out of town.

It was nearing eleven by the time Eli and his group gathered along the state highway. From their location, the lush green foliage of June obscured Chinamans Bluff. With some assistance, Eli fashioned a cane from a fallen branch he found near the edge of the highway. Using this makeshift staff to steady himself, he pushed forward. The group began walking as a column deep into the forest before breaking off in intervals of fifty feet or so. Finished, they formed an irregular phalanx of over one thousand yards. Once Eli gave the command, from his midpoint spot in the string of searchers, the volunteers moved forward. The line ebbed and flowed, trying to maintain visual contact when possible and voice communication when not.

Hoots and hollers punctuated the air along with the wild thrashing of the brush. Stirred before the moving formation, birds took flight, deer along with their fawn, scattered. The thicket beneath their feet crackled, and the soil rising under tramping boots clung to their overalls. As the group approached Chinamans Bluff, the faint outline of its crest was barely visible beyond the woodland's canopy's rich latticework.

The distant shouting of Miles Gunter's group, approaching from the south, could be heard. "Pass the word," Eli yelled to each of his flanks, "Have everyone start gathering around the bluff." His command reverberated down both edges of the line.

Once Eli reached the clearing at the bluff's base, his thoughts were of Lucy and the night they made love. Despite the presence of all the volunteers that pressed around him, he felt alone within his feelings. It wasn't until Miles asked for advice did he begin to come out of his trance.

"We followed Vincent's trail," Miles said with conviction. He pointed upward. "I'm certain he's hiding up there. What's the plan?"

Eli heard but was preoccupied, and his detachment evident.

"What d'ya think we should do? Miles probed again.

"Yeah," Eli replied coolly. "There's only one way up. I think that I should be the one to get him."

"You sure?" asked Miles, clearly troubled by Eli's plan.

"Yeah, I'll go by myself. I don't want the kid to panic. I'll ease him down."

"But your arm?"

"I'll be fine." Eli started to make his way toward the slope, and the crowd eased back.

He jammed his staff into the slope and pushed his way up. With each step, tension began to build in him. It was a slow process, not so much because of the terrain, but because he questioned his ability for restraint. It was a matter of fear of himself.

## 41

The mid-day sun streamed down on Eli when he reached the top of the ridge. Vincent was nowhere to be seen. Besides the twisted clusters of tenacious scrub pine that clung stubbornly to the sandstone bluff, the plateau appeared unoccupied. He noted that some of the grimmia moss that carpeted the surface had been recently disturbed. The bright red patches of British Soldier Lichen that once relaxed peacefully within its plush green blanket had been compressed. The well-defined outline of a shoe revealed the source of its destruction.

"Vincent," Eli called out. "I know you're here."

Silence.

Although the top of the bluff was comparatively flat, the eons of weathering sculpted its shell into steps and ridges, making walking near the edges unsafe.

"Vincent, come out. I want to hear what happened."

Silence.

"Your mother is worried sick."

Silence."

Eli saw several Turkey Vultures lazily circle high overhead. He continued to advance toward the center of the bluff.

"Vincent!" he called out louder. "Your mom wants you to come home. Was it an accident?"

Silence.

As Eli traveled beyond the midpoint, he caught a glimpse of a blue checkered flannel shirt alarmingly close to the edge. The shirt moved.

Now closer to Vincent, Eli softened his voice. "I see where you are. You're too close to the edge."

Vincent raised his head. He stretched his arms onto the ledge. Scratched and soiled, channels of sand-fused tears lined his face.

Eli froze. Seeing his pitiful state turned his vengeful heart to pity. "Vincent, come away from the ledge."

"No! You're gonna hurt me," he blubbered.

Eli moved closer.

"Stop!" Vincent shouted.

"Okay." Eli discarded his staff and raised his hands in submission. "Can you tell me what happened?"

"It was an accident. I was pretending to be a newspaper reporter."

"A reporter?"

"Yes. Mrs. Perkins said I was her cub reporter."

The explanation stunned Eli. "Who? Why? Why did you go into Lucy's room?"

Vincent shook his head contritely. "I'm sorry. I'm sorry. I didn't mean to hurt her. I... I was only getting information for Mrs. Perkins."

Eli rubbed the back of his neck. "What does Olive Perkins have to do with all this?"

Vincent began to cry. He shifted in place, and his feet moved slightly beyond the ledge. "She said, I... I could have a byline in the paper."

"For snooping on Lucy?"

"Sort of." Vincent began to pull himself onto the ledge.

Eli saw Vincent was having a difficult time gaining traction. He went over to him and extended his right arm.

Vincent tried to bring his left knee onto the outcropping. Unbalanced by the sudden shift in his body, he reached out in panic to grab Eli. Vincent's moist fingers slipped past Eli's hand while Vincent's arms flayed powerlessly against the loose sand.

Helpless, Eli witnessed Vincent's terror-filled eyes disappear from view.

## 42

D r. George Brewer kept vigil with Helen after Vincent's body arrived at the Spencer house. He tended to her needs and joined her in welcoming mourners who began to pass through the front parlor. Besides the condolences, many women brought with them an assortment of food.

"Oh, Helen, please accept my deepest sympathy," many said with tear-filled eyes. Some would embrace her before going over to the open casket to view the body and then file it out through the kitchen. Some stayed, taking turns at consoling and helping with the food. At times, Helen would attempt to rise from her couch. The weight of her sorrow caused Helen's legs to buckle, forcing her back down. The procession continued until Helen succumbed to utter fatigue.

"Why don't you go to bed and take a nap for a while?" Dr. Brewer offered.

"No," she protested. "I want to stay with my baby."

Despite her determination to stay awake, she could no longer fight the exhaustion and fell into a deep slumber. Once Dr. Brewer saw to it that Helen was comfortable, he moved to one of the Queen Anne chairs across the room. He placed an ottoman in front of it, propped up his legs, then fell fast asleep.

THE DAY of Vincent's funeral was warm and sunny; ordinarily, the kind of day that would be welcomed and appreciated for its pleasantness. Now clothed in a black dress, Helen opened the door for the funeral director to take Vincent into the black Packard Henney Hearse. As the casket cleared the front doorway, Helen wailed. George Brewer held her tightly.

"My Baby! Why? Oh, why," she moaned.

Dr. Brewer helped Helen into his car then followed the hearse to the Methodist church. Without a word, they followed Vincent's casket down the aisle then took their place at the front pew. Other mourners, beginning with the back row, filed past the open casket before returning to their seats. The funeral director and an aide closed the casket.

In the long, uneasy silence that trailed after the last person returned to their pews, the pastor walked to the pulpit.

Pastor Rowland Tillett, a tall, bespectacled man in his mid-fifties with balding grey hair, looked out over the congregation with a humble demeanor. He quietly cleared his throat. "Friends, we have gathered here to praise God and to witness to our faith as we celebrate the life of Vincent Randolf Spencer. We come together in grief, acknowledging our human loss. May God grant us grace, that in pain, we may find comfort, in sorrow hope, and in death resurrection."

The choir immediately began to sing, "In the sweet goodbye and goodbye" amid sobs and outcries of anguish. As the last note faded, Pastor Tillett launched into an emotional eulogy on the life of Vincent. Helen, fixed on every word, appeared to glow with heart-rending contentment as he shared Vincent's life with the gathering.

Finished, the pastor nodded to the choir. They began to sing, "Shall we gather at the river?"

A new round of kerchief-muffled cries began.

Pastor Tillett then stood before the casket and said, "Almighty God, be with us as we set off on this journey—this journey which is not only measured in miles but also measured in tears and memories.

As we enter the valley of the shadow of death, be to us our Good Shepard, as you promised."

Aided by Dr. Brewer, Helen began the slow recessional out of the church and to the gravesite.

## 43

E verett Jackson, bulbous-nosed, rotund, and bar-room ruddy, entered the front of the courtroom after the noon lunch break. Acting in his position as the duly elected coroner, he took his place. His wife, functioning as the recorder, sat at a nearby table.

The courthouse in Morrisville bulged to capacity. Persons involved in the testimony concerning Lucy Lareau's deaths and Vincent Spencer occupied the two front rows. Only six men sat in the jury's box. Dressed in an assortment of bib-overalls with chambray shirts, white dress shirts with broad suspenders to hold up their britches, they appeared uneasy. A couple of men wore light summer suits. The sea of waving fans and straw hats ineffectively pushed around the muggy July air. Those unable to enter filled the hallway with hopes of gleaning any testimony that happened to trickle out.

A hush descended when the coroner called Eli Buchanan. "Please take a seat in the witness chair, Mr. Buchanan."

Eli sat down and nervously scanned the room. He caught sight of Sheriff Frank Dawson sitting next to Eli's ex-wife, Barbara.

"Do you swear to tell the truth, the whole truth, so help you, God?"

"I do."

"Please state your full name."

"Eli James Buchanan."

"Mr. Buchanan, what is your position in Chandlers Bend?" the coroner asked offishly.

"I am the town's constable."

"And where were you on the day that Miss Lucy Lareau died?"

"I... I was in my office."

"Mr. Buchanan, how were you informed of the shooting?"

"I received a call from Hulda Brown, the operator employed by the Lindman Telephone Company, that Lucy Lareau had been shot."

"And what did you do?"

"I straightaway got into my car and went over to Helen's house."

"Mr. Buchanan, just tell us what you saw immediately after reaching the second story of Mrs. Helen Spencer's house."

Eli looked at Helen, who was in the front row and blotting tears from her eyes. "I ran up the stairs and found Helen... ah, Mrs. Spencer crying over Miss Lareau's body."

"Was she holding a gun?" the coroner asked bluntly.

Eli shook his head. "No, sir."

"Did you see any gun when you entered the room?"

"I had just entered through the doorway when I saw what appeared to be a Colt automatic pistol. It was lying near Miss Lareau's body."

The coroner held up a gun. "Is this the weapon that you saw?"

"Yes, sir."

"For the record, it will be noted that the weapon involved is a .32 caliber Colt model 1903 hammerless pocket pistol, with serial numbers 505632. What happened next, Mr. Buchanan?"

"I fell to my knees. I held Lucy in my arms," Eli said with a halting voice.

There were a few sobs heard from those in attendance.

"Mr. Buchanan, for the record, what was your relationship with Lucy Lareau?"

Eli looked down at his trembling hands. "She was my girlfriend."

"What happened next?"

"I don't remember too much. I guess that I tried to revive Lucy, then Doctor Brewer came in and took over."

"What did he do?"

"He knelt beside me. Using his stethoscope, he listened for Lucy's heartbeat."

"And then what happened?"

"I became angry. I wanted to know how this could have happened?"

"Who did you ask?"

"Helen," Eli said softly.

"What did she tell you?"

"She said that Vincent, her son, had something to do with it."

The coroner, appearing relaxed up to this point, turned more directly toward Eli. "What was your first impulse after hearing that?"

"I wanted to ..." Eli appeared to check himself. "I wanted to get him."

"I understand you organized a search party."

"Yes, sir. I took a couple of dozen men, or so, with me and went north of Chinamans Bluff to circle back south. I asked Miles Gunter to lead a group out of town—going north."

"And what was the plan?" the coroner asked, his voice rising.

Eli shifted. "The plan was to trap Vincent between our two groups."

"Prior to the time of the search party, Dr. Brewer testified, in his words that he told you, 'I think you should let Sheriff Dawson handle this.' Is that correct?"

Eli glanced at the jury. "Yeah."

"So, Mr. Buchannan, why didn't you."

"I took his suggestion to mean the handling of the crime scene."

"Okay, Mr. Buchannan, now you did organize a search party and discovered Vincent at Chinamans Bluff."

"Yes, sir. We found him at Chinamans Bluff."

"Mr. Buchanan, when you say that 'we found him,' you mean that you're the one who actually found him. Isn't that right?"

"Yes, sir."

An audible sigh of unease filled the courtroom.

"Ladies and gentlemen, if there are further outbursts, I will have the bailiff clear the courtroom." The chatterings ceased. Only the swooshing sound of makeshift fans lingered.

"Where did you find Vincent, Mr. Buchanan?"

"I found him on top of Chinamans Bluff, lyin' down on an outcropping near the edge."

"Considering that there were several dozen people with you, why were you the only one to go up the bluff?"

"I was afraid that Vincent would panic. I wanted to talk to him, one-on-one."

"So, what did he say?"

Eli shook his head in puzzlement. "First off, he said it was an accident that he shot Lucy Lareau. He then started to blame Olive Perkins."

There was a collective gasp.

Olive Perkins, who up to this point, was busy taking notes, froze. She looked around the room in confusion.

All eyes silently interrogated her.

## 44

"Mr. Buchannan, that is news to this inquest. What did Olive Perkins have to do with the death of Lucy Lareau?"

Olive Perkins squirmed.

Eli shrugged. "I don't know."

The coroner leaned forward on his desk. Keeping his eyes on Olive, he asked, "Mr. Buchannan, what exactly did Vincent say regarding Olive Perkins."

"Vincent told me that Mrs. Perkins was going to give him a byline in the *Chandlers Bend Telegraph* newspaper."

"For snooping around Miss Lareau's room?" the coroner asked incredulously.

"I don't know. For some reason, Vincent was under the impression that something in her room was going to give him a byline."

"Did Vincent say anything more?"

"No, sir. The outcropping was very narrow that he was lying on. Vincent started to pull himself up to the next level. I saw he was having a difficult time, so I went to give him a hand."

"Then what happened?"

"Vincent started to slip. I rushed over to him. He reached out to me with damp hands. They just slid off mine. I couldn't get a grip."

Helen Spencer burst into tears.

A palpable lament of sympathy filled the courtroom.

"What happened next?"

"I yelled, 'Vincent' and rushed to the edge of the bluff and looked down. Several men from the search party quickly gathered around him. He wasn't moving."

"Witness excused," announced the coroner formally.

AFTER A BREAK IN THE PROCEEDINGS, Everett Jackson resumed his position. "Will Olive Perkins, please come forward and take the witness stand."

Hesitant and measured, Olive moved to the front of the courtroom and sat down timidly.

After administering the oath, the coroner said, "Please state your full name and occupation."

"My name is Olive Jean Perkins. I am the co-owner and reporter for the *Chandlers Bend Telegraph* newspaper."

"Mrs. Perkins, what is your relationship with the deceased, Vincent Spencer?"

"He is... ah, he was my newspaper delivery boy."

"How long did you employ him?"

Olive paused and appeared to search her memory. "About five years."

"What sort of person was Vincent?"

"He was a very nice boy," Olive said, choking on her words.

"In your opinion, do you think Vincent was capable of killing anyone?"

Olive gasped. "Of course not! He was a sweet boy."

"Mrs. Perkins, besides being a newspaper boy, was Vincent a reporter for your newspaper?"

"No, sir."

"Then, why do you think he told Mr. Buchanan that he was a reporter?"

Olive squirmed.

"Mrs. Perkins, please answer the question."

"I... I... ah, I sort of told Vincent he would be my cub reporter."

"Did you pay him for that job?"

"No, sir."

"Why was Vincent snooping around in Lucy Lareau's room?"

"I have no idea," Olive cried.

"According to Mr. Buchanan, Vincent mentioned you as the reason he was in her room. Can you shed some light on why?"

"I'll tell you what I told him. I said that if he wanted to be a reporter, he had to snoop around for news. You know, dig around. All I can guess is that he felt there was some kind of story there. She was relatively new in town. There was a lot of speculation about her, and I suppose he ... well, you know. Kids have big imaginations."

"Mrs. Perkins, did he ever mention anything in particular about Lucy Lareau?

"No, sir."

"The witness is excused."

Olive felt Helen Spencer's killing glare as she walked back to her seat.

"This hearing is adjourned until Friday, the twenty-seventh, at which time I will issue my report."

## 45

Once again, the Morrisville Court House was brimming with spectators. Necks craned, and attendees stirred as Coroner Everett Jackson entered the front of the courtroom. The warmness of the July morning accompanied all those present as they ineffectively tried to keep it at bay by brandishing any object they could lay their hands on to fan themselves. The men seated in the jury box, having experienced the grueling heat from their last session, unanimously appeared to have preferred white dress shirts as a more fitting attire to accompany their assortment of plaid, herringbone, and striped trousers.

Everett Jackson cleared his throat and hammered the gavel onto his desk in an assertive manner.

"This inquest will come to order."

Several more smacks of the mallet were needed to bring the gathering to attention. His dictatorial comportment achieved results while losing approval from some of the more sensitive.

"This inquest will come to order," Jackson began. "Due to the unique coincidence of the deaths of Vincent Spencer and Lucy Lareau, I will be issuing my conclusion on both cases sequentially."

A hush descended on the assembly.

Retrieving his spectacles from his shirt pocket, Everett Jackson donned them with some difficulty before lifting the report off his desk. "In the matter of Lucy Lareau, who died on June 23, 1934—I hereby conclude she died as a result of a single bullet to her heart. After hearing the testimony of all persons involved, I further rule that the motive for her death remains inconclusive."

The shock of the news rippled through the courthouse like dry leaves driven by a late Autumn gust. As everyone murmured amongst themselves, their disbelief routed the slightest concern over the summer's heat.

Again, Coroner Jackson hammered his gavel on his desk.

"Order in the courtroom!"

His stern gaze moved throughout the room, silencing the unruly. Once calm was restored, he resumed. "In the matter of Vincent Spencer, who died on June 23, 1934; I do hereby conclude he died as a result of a fall, causing the abdominal aorta to rupture. He also sustained damage to the bowels, liver, and kidneys, which resulted in internal bleeding. After hearing the testimony of all persons involved, I rule his death to be the result of an accidental fall off Chinamans Bluff."

Everett Jackson looked toward the jury. "Having investigated the deaths of Lucy Lareau and Vincent Spencer, I make the following recommendations to the jury that my finding is accepted as read. If there are any objections, will those challenging my findings please raise their hands right now?"

All jurors fidgeted without raising any objections.

Following a tense silence, Everett Jackson removed a kerchief from a pocket and wiped his brow. "Because there is no proof that Vincent Spencer acted with the requisite criminal intent, it cannot be proven beyond a reasonable doubt that he intentionally fired the .32 caliber Colt Model 1903 pistol. Therefore, for the reasons set forth above, this matter should be closed." Hitting the gavel once, he declared, "This inquest is closed."

## 46

Having selected a spot at the rear of the room, Eli Buchanan eagerly left the warm courthouse ahead of the rest of the attendees. Pushing past those in the outer hall, he was one of the first to make it outside. Purposely avoiding eye contact with any of the others, Eli made a beeline for his Buick Coupé. As he drove away, he caught a glimpse of Olive Perkins and thankful she was unable to hound him for his reaction.

With his windows rolled down, the continual rush of air swirled madly around the interior of the car as his foot pressed forcefully on the gas pedal. Eli tried to think about the wild days of running booze, but the phantom memories of Lucy could not be driven from his mind as effortlessly as the wind. He glanced at the empty seat, and immediately, his eyes filled with tears. It wasn't until he reached Chandlers Bend that his weeping abated.

Eli began to head to his office to get drunk but changed course for Helen Spencer's house. He killed the engine and sat there for a long time before getting out. With dread, he reluctantly knocked on Helen's front door. Eli heard approaching footsteps.

The front door's curtain was pushed back, and he saw Helen's sad face looking back at him.

The speech Eli had mentally prepared dissipated before her grieving eyes.

"Come in," she said vacantly.

Without a word, Eli followed her into the kitchen.

Helen motioned toward one of the chairs. "Sit there, if you like."

He grabbed the chair and sat. "I... I—"

"I think I know why you're here." She chose the chair on the opposite side. "I'll tell you right now. I feel emotionally drained. Over the last three weeks, I've cried myself dry. My Vincent is gone, and my reason for living died with him, too. If you've come to say you're sorry, I don't blame you."

Eli shook his head. "You may not, but I blame myself for not being able to grab Vincent in time."

Helen reached out and patted his hand. "There's only one person to blame, and that is Olive Perkins. If it weren't for her filling Vincent's head with that reporter stuff, none of this would have ever happened."

Eli looked down at the table. "I came here to apologize and ask for your forgiveness."

Helen grabbed both of his hands. He looked up at her.

"What's done is done. All the crying in the world isn't going to bring my Vincent back. And besides, you have your own loss to deal with."

Eli nodded.

Helen let go of her hold on his hands. "I noticed the other day that you got rid of that sling, but you were gone before I could ask how you were doing."

"Yeah. It's fine now. I think I may have pushed it a bit, but George said it's okay."

"Did you go to the coroner's inquest this morning?" Helen asked.

"Yeah. Yeah, I did."

"I couldn't put myself through that nightmare anymore. I heard enough. Was anything new said?"

"Uh-huh."

"About Vincent?"

"Yeah, Everett Jackson said the motive for Lucy's death was inconclusive."

"Inconclusive? What does that mean?" Helen asked furiously.

"Well, it came down to motive. Jackson said, based on the testimony, it was doubtful that Vincent acted with criminal intent."

She fumed. "You're darn right he didn't."

Eli waited for Helen to calm down. "The upshot of it all is that Vincent won't be considered a murderer."

She sat back in her chair and crossed her arms. "I hate this town, this county, and all the people in it."

Eli felt the sting of her words.

"Oh, I'm sorry. I didn't mean everybody," Helen said remorsefully.

"That's all right. I know what you mean. I kinda feel the same way."

"What did they have to say about Lucy?"

"Nothing much, just that she died of a gunshot wound to her heart."

"Where is Lucy going to be buried?" Helen asked softly.

"Right now, no one has claimed the body. I'm going to ask the coroner for her remains. I'll see to it that she gets a proper burial."

"When you do, let me know."

Eli sighed. "I will. I better get going. Thank you."

"Ah... Eli. Before you go, could you do me a favor?"

Eli rose. "Sure, what do you need?"

"George cleaned up Lucy's room and got rid of the rug and bed covers. I haven't been able to go into it myself. Do you suppose you could take her stuff and give it to someone in need? I don't trust anyone else, except George, but he's done a lot for me already. Maybe there's some token of hers you want to keep?"

"I understand, Helen. Do you have any boxes that I can use?"

"I don't think you'll need them. Lucy had two suitcases when she arrived. You'll probably find them in the closet."

## 47

The heaviness of his sadness and the sour smell of the slaying confronted Eli as he slowly opened the door to Lucy's room. His spirits were indeed weighty and more sensitive, but the pong of death was tangible. The airless room, sealed like a tomb, trapped the traces of the past. Eli went to the window and raised the sash. A current of air flowed past him as he surveyed the interior.

Eli looked at the bloodstained wood flooring that marked the spot where Lucy died. He redirected to the pinewood dressing bureau. A comb, brush, and an ornate hand mirror lay haphazardly on its surface. Eli picked up the brush and noted a few blonde hairs fixed to its bristles. He meditatively ran his hand over its coarse surface, then set it aside, more captivated by the hand mirror. The handle was an intertwining pattern of light green and vibrant purple stems with white Calla Lilys against a lush background of leaves. When he flipped it over, there was a carved butterfly perched on its rim, its colorful dorsal wing partially draping over the mirror's surface. He carefully placed it on the exposed mattress.

Trapped in maudlin reflections, Eli shook off his musings and turned to the task of removing Lucy's things. He went into the closet and proceeded to stack clothes on the bed. Remembering what Helen said, he spotted two suitcases on the top shelf. Using the small footstool that lay off to the side, Eli removed the cases and set them on the floor. When he handled the brown and tan striped tweed suitcase, it felt more substantial. Although smaller, he detected a shift of something inside.

Curious, Eli lifted the case and placed it over Lucy's clothing. He tried pushing the slide catches, but they wouldn't budge. Eli lifted the bag and shook it several times to confirm that there was something inside. The latches did not appear to be anything unusual, so he flipped open the awl on his pocket knife. Using it as an improvised key, he successfully undid the lock.

Eli was no stranger to a leather and canvas bank bag. Unlike those he was familiar with, the markings on it were obliterated. Eli opened the sack and peered inside. Surprised with what he saw, he hurriedly dumped the contents into the suitcase. Bundles of cash rained down like fodder into a feeding trough. He flung the bag aside and stared at the assortment of bills.

The thought occurred to him to put everything back, place all of Lucy's possessions into the bags, and leave.

*No one would be the wiser.*

Then he thought about Helen, her loss—her future. He wasn't going to make the same mistake he made with the bank robbery haul. He turned away and headed downstairs.

"Helen," Eli called out even before reaching the bottom floor.

"I'm in the kitchen," she responded dully.

Eli found her working over the kitchen sink. "You need to come upstairs."

Helen shook her head. "I can't. I really can't go into that room right now. Besides, what's so important for me to see?"

He raised his hands in obedience. "Okay, I'll bring it down to you," he said before running back upstairs.

Once Eli was back in Lucy's room, he hastily shoved the money back into the bank bag and hurried back to the kitchen.

"What's that?" she asked.

"It's a banker's bag," he said before dumping the cash onto the table.

Helen gasped. "Where did you find that?"

"It was in one of Lucy's suitcases."

"Where did she get that kind of money?" she asked in disbelief.

"I haven't the slightest idea. There aren't any markings on the bands around the money. Did Lucy ever say anything about having a large amount of money?"

"I wonder if it has something to do with that guy she was supposed to meet?"

"What guy?"

"Oh, I probably shouldn't have said anything. Now, this is the God's honest truth. Before she started seeing you, she had a boyfriend. His name was John."

"That's it? John?"

Helen nodded. "She never said his last name. Lucy told me that he was supposed to meet her—right here in Chandlers Bend."

"What happened?"

"I don't know. One day she's pining for him, the next day, she has a good cry, and she's over it—just like that."

"If it's something to do with this money, I suspect the guy's probably dead. You don't leave that kind of money behind."

Helen, wide-eyed, sat down and stared at the pile. "How much do you think is there?"

"Don't really know, without counting it. If I were to guess, I'd say … ah, maybe twenty thousand bucks. Maybe more."

"What do we do with it?"

Standing next to the table with his hands on his hips, Eli remained quiet.

"Eli?" Helen prodded.

Unresponsive at first, he sat down on the opposite side of the table from Helen. "I think we should do nothing," he said quietly.

"What?"

With a slow, measured retort, he said, "We should keep this to ourselves."

"But … I …" She stopped in midthought.

"Maybe this is a lot to take in right now. You need to let this digest." Eli began to collect the money from the table and return it to the bag. "I'm going to put this back where I found it. I'll take care of the rest of Lucy's things."

Helen nodded and appeared lost in thought.

## 48

D r. Brewer shuffled listlessly around his small waiting room, getting organized for the day's load of patients. He routinely raised shades to let in the morning light, then straightened a few chairs before unlocking the front door. When he went into his office and saw the neat stacks of folders on his desk, he thought of Lucy. Doc remembered the liveliness she brought into his life. He heard the entry door's bell ring.

He cracked open the office door. "Good morning, Ida. I'll be out in a minute."

"Sure thing, Doc. Good morning to ya, too. Don't mind me. I'll be about me business."

He closed the door and sat down in front of his desk. It wasn't that he had a lot of paperwork to do. It was more of retreating from the world, even if it was only minutes. When he heard the call of the bell again, he knew his respite was over.

Sally O'Dell sat patiently with her son Bobby. When Doc approached Sally, he saw that her left eye was discolored and swollen.

"Sally, what happened to you?"

She forced a smile. "Oh, clumsy me. Took a bit of a wee tumble down the stairs."

Doc sensed her uneasiness.

He looked at her son. "Hey, Bobby. How are you doing?"

"Fine, Dr. Brewer." Bobby produced a copy of *Treasure Island* from a canvas sack. "Thanks for letting me read this book. Mom helped me with the hard words." He held out the book.

Dr. Brewer waved it away. "I'll tell you what. You can keep that and start your own library."

Bobby quickly retracted the book. "Thanks," he said, smiling enthusiastically.

"And before you go, I have another one you can add to that collection. Now, Sally, we can talk about Bobby's leg in a minute, but first, why don't you come into my office so I can have a look at that eye."

Sally shook her head. "No, it's fine, Doc. I just came here for Bobby."

Dr. Brewer reached out. "C'mon. Let me have a look at that in my office."

Bobby, his pegged leg motionless while the other leg rhythmically swung back and forth, looked up as Dr. Brewer took his mother by the hand. He gave him a wink, which Bobby countered with a smile.

Once Sally was sitting in his office, he examined her eye a little closer. Doc gently pushed down on the affected area. "Hum, does this hurt?"

"A little."

He increased the pressure.

"Ouch!" she cried out.

"I'm sorry. Are you experiencing any dizziness or double vision?"

"No."

He went to the icebox and chipped off a piece of ice. Wrapping it in a cloth, Doc gave it to Sally. "Here, put this on that eye."

As Sally held the icepack in place, he took a seat opposite of her. "Sally, that isn't from falling down the stairs."

She averted his probing gaze.

"Peter did that to you, didn't he?"

"He didn't mean it, Doc. We were just having—"

"Listen to me, Sally. You could have been seriously injured. In fact, you may have lost the use of that eye. I'm going to have a talk with him."

"Oh, no. Please, Doc ... let me handle this myself."

Dr. Brewer abruptly rose. He scoffed, "Like you handled this?"

"Doc, you'll only make matters worse. Pete's under a lot of pressure. You know... the economy and the mill is having a hard time competing with the big mills in the Twin Cities. He's a good man, Doc."

He remained quiet and went over to a side table where he unwrapped a new pegleg. "I'm going to go and get Bobby. Keep that icepack on your eye for a few more minutes."

Dr. Brewer brought Bobby in and helped him onto the side table. "Bobby, when I told Ed Sanders that you needed a new leg, he carved this one especially for you. When I told him that I gave you *Treasure Island* to read, he said he would carve something special into it."

Bobby's eyes sparkled as he gawked at his new prosthetic leg. "Wow, there's anchors, ships, and birds," he shouted gleefully.

"Ed Sanders is a friend of mine. He used to be in the navy, so he knows a lot about the ocean and sailing. He told me that when he was at sea, he would pass the time carving. So, he figured you would like something nautical."

"Wow! This is really special. I really like it."

Sally rose from her chair and took a closer look. "That's amazing, Doc, but I don't think I can afford it."

"Don't worry about it. Ed did it for Bobby as a gift. He told me that sailors used to carve into ivory. They called it scrimshaw."

Sally picked up the leg and carefully examined it. "This is excellent work. Bobby, you're going to have to write Mr. Sanders a nice thank you letter."

Bobby nodded. "I will, Mama."

"Okay, Bobby, now let's get that on you so you can show it off."

Once fitted with the new leg, Doc gave him a copy of *Swallows and*

*Amazons.* "Now you go home and read this book. It's all about the sea."

Both Sally and Bobby left the office with broad smiles.

Dr. Brewer saw that his waiting room was empty except for Ida, who was busy cleaning the windows. "Ida, I have to go down to Adams Creek. If anybody needs me and don't mind waitin', I'll be back in about an hour."

The ride to the grist mill took only fifteen minutes, but the anger that seethed in Dr. Brewer's heart grew disproportionately to the distance.

Scoured by the harsh extremes of midwest weather and unkempt because of expense in a struggling economy, Knudtson's Mill was a monument to a passing generation. With timbers bleached by time into greyish bones, the unembellished building looked abandoned except for the workmen who labored within its decrepit hulk. Only its water wheel remained motionless.

Aaren Knudtson, tall and wrinkled, stood scrutinizing his employees from his roost near the curve of the wheel. One foot rested on the guardrail in monarch stateliness. His aging features matched those of his mill. Having arrived from Norway fifty-some years ago with his young wife, he saw the need for a grist mill in the growing farming community around Chandlers Bend. Mindful of saving a penny to grow more pennies, his tight-fistedness was legendary, known for extracting more labor than wages paid. He stood erect when Dr. Brewer's car pulled up.

Dr. Brewer got out of his vehicle and waved a greeting. Aaren Knudtson was old, but he had a liveliness in his stride and hurried down the ramp steps that led to the dirt road below.

"Vat brings ya here, Doc?" Knudtson asked.

"I need to talk to Pete O'Dell."

"Somethin' vrong with da misses?"

Dr. Brewer shook his head. "No, nothing like that, Aaren. I'll only be a minute."

Doc saw suspicion written on Knudtson's face. "Vell ... if ya only gonna be a minute. I suppose ..." he trailed off, his stumbling voice revealing puzzlement.

"Where is he working?"

Reluctantly, Knudtson pointed toward the open double-door at the top of the incline. "Pete's vorking on da separator. Gettin' ready vor harvest."

Dr. Brewer tipped his hat and walked past Aaren.

Thin rays of sunlight cut through the shadowy interior, where the grain dust hovered lazily. Through the dim cloud, he spotted Peter O'Dell, the only one in that room, hunched over the sifter.

Dr. Brewer walked over and stood next to him until Peter took note of his presence.

"Hey, Doc. What brings ya here?"

As Peter O'Dell straightened up, Doc gave him a haymaker against his left temple, sending him crashing to the floor. Looking bewildered, Pete tried to lift himself, but Doc used his foot to push him back down. "Stay down, you son-of-a-bitch,"

Peter rubbed the side of his head. "Whaddaya do that for?"

Pointing an accusatory finger, he said, "If you ever lay a hand on Sally again, I'll do more than that."

Peter glared at him. "Ya ain't gonna tell me how to treat me wife."

A rage began to percolate inside George Brewer that he hadn't felt since his war years. He looked around and spotted an abandoned ax handle. He removed his foot from Peter's chest and went over to pick it up. Holding it over his shoulder like a baseball player sporting a bat, he rushed toward Peter.

Peter shuffled backward, his arms and feet moving like a crab, eyes wide with panic. "You're crazy!" he yelled.

"Shut up, you bastard!" Dr. Brewer drew back but checked himself. "If you ever hurt your wife again, I'll show you how crazy I am. You got that?"

Peter vigorously nodded his head and raised a defensive hand. "Got it," he sputtered back.

"And if you mentioned my visit to Sally, you'll hear from me. Understood?"

"Yeah," Peter mumbled.

Doc flung the handle aside and turned to walk out just as Aaren Knudtson came into the sifting room.

Peter O'Dell scrambled to his feet.

"Vat's going on?" Knudtson asked, looking uneasily at the men.

Dr. Brewer didn't reply but continued to move toward the open-air and down to his car.

# 49

Helen Spenser was aimlessly looking over skeins of yarn in the back of Chandler's General Store when Mildrid Lowe and Caroline Dunlop walked in. Both women appeared engaged in a spirited conversation that continued into the store. Neither of them noticed Helen.

"I know, it's a mystery to me, too, why a young boy like Vincent should even be in a woman's bedroom," cackled Caroline.

"I tell you, there were some strange things going on in that Spencer household," Mildrid chimed in.

"Yeah, I saw them, all so cozy, sitting together at the village dances," Caroline announced obtrusively.

Susanna Chandler, hearing the chatter, strolled over to greet them. "Good morning. What's so important that has you two ladies in such a tizzy?"

"We were at the final inquest at the Morrisville Court House. Inconclusive, in a pig's eye, I say," snapped Mildred. "If I was making a decision, knowing what I know, I—"

"Ahem!" Susanna cleared her throat loudly.

Helen heard the entire exchange and saw Susanna cock her head in her direction to indicate Helen's presence.

Coming around her concealment of shelving, cluttered with an assortment of housewares, Helen strode defiantly past the assembly. She gave each one a glower of contempt.

Shamefacedly, they averted their eyes and appeared to examine the store's goods.

When Helen heard the bell chime as she exited, she swore to herself that would be the last time. She scanned the few motley inhabitants of the town who were walking down the street of Chandlers Bend. Although dissimilar in appearance, Helen felt there was a commonality of heart. While they had shown sympathy at Vincent's funeral, on the one hand, their gossipy lips were full of maliciousness.

Now that he was laid to rest, they adopted an indifferent attitude, she thought, no doubt fueled by the likes of Mildrid Lowe and Caroline Dunlop.

Without purpose in her wanderings except to walk off her anger, Helen's route led her to Eli's office. Before trying the doorknob, she knocked and heard his voice.

Eli, sober-faced, leaned back in his chair, his feet propped on top of his desk, and arms locked over his chest. "Well, this is a surprise," he said as his feet dropped to the floor and sat to attention. He then leaned forward and rested his arms on top of his desk.

Helen grabbed the chair on the other side of his desk and sat down.

"You look upset," Eli said, appearing to study her.

"I just came from Chandler's store. I'm never setting foot in that place again."

"What happened?"

"Mildrid Lowe, Caroline Dunlop, and Susanna Chandler. That place is a viper's nest of rumormongers," she bawled.

"Something they said?"

Helen shook her head. "It doesn't matter," she said listlessly. "The whole town has been infected by their poison. They sit in an angelic pose in church yet cannot tame their tongues, full of their venomous words."

"So, are you having second thoughts about the money?"

"Maybe. I didn't come here with that in mind. I only stopped because I happened ..." She trailed off and looked with pleading eyes at Eli. "I don't know what to think anymore."

"I don't know what to think, either. I intended to stop by your house later today and tell you that the coroner is releasing Lucy's body. I'll have a private graveside service this coming Friday. I was hoping you would be there."

"I already told you that I would. What time is the burial?"

"Ten. I don't know if Lucy belonged to any church, but the Methodist minister said he would perform the service. I haven't spread the news. Besides the two of us, the pastor and the gravediggers are probably going to be the only ones."

"Eli, you know you can't keep a secret in Chandlers Bend. There's a pair of snooping eyes behind every lace curtain in this damn town."

"I know what you mean. I think the townsfolk are too embarrassed by their spying to be there. Oh, they'll see, like you said behind their curtains, but they won't show their faces."

"What about Doc?" Helen asked. "If it's okay with you, may I invite him? I'm certain he'll come."

Eli nodded. "Sure, of course, I forgot about George. And speaking about Doc, have you said anything to him about the money?"

"No, I considered that our secret?"

"Good. You probably know that Doc's kinda sweet on you."

"Yeah, I know."

"You're not happy about that?"

"Maybe a month or two ago, I would have felt differently, but after Vincent's death and the backbiting ... things aren't the same."

"Don't you think people will have a different attitude toward you if you and George were to get married?"

"Frankly, Eli, no. They may be more discreet, but I'll be forever known as the mother of a killer. You see, the word 'inconclusive' gives people a lot of wiggle-room for malicious gossip. Besides, George never really indicated that he wants to marry me. We just didn't have the time to know each other before all of this stuff happened." Helen felt the anger and grief boiling inside her.

"From what I observed, he cares for you."

"Eli, it may be more sympathy than love." She pulled out a kerchief and blotted her eyes, "I'm not going to have someone marry me out of pity."

There was a silent uneasiness in the room only interrupted by the rattle of moving vehicles traveling past the jailhouse.

Helen sighed. "What about you, Eli? I have the feeling you're not happy here, either."

Eli straightened in his chair. "I've been thinking about heading to the Dakotas."

"Dakotas?"

"Yep. I know what you're thinking, but they need lawmen to help keep order. Despite the lousy weather, the drought, and all that, I think it best for me to move on. I even heard there's some talk of forming a State Highway Patrol in North Dakota."

"Another lawman's job?"

Eli shrugged. "It's in my blood."

Helen shifted in her chair. "I hear it's pretty bad. Lots of farmers are losing their land, and from what the newspapers are saying, it turns violent when their places go on the auction block."

Eli leaned back in his chair and cupped his hands behind his head. "Yeah, I know... maybe they could use a sympathetic sheriff. You know, someone who wouldn't try to—"

Helen smiled and cut him off. "Eli, you may think you're a lawman, but you got a soft spot behind that badge of yours. I'm not so sure you're cut out for that kind of work like what's going on in the Dakotas."

"You might be right, Helen. But like you, I'm not comfortable staying in this town."

"Eli, you know that's a lot of money Lucy left behind. I'm thinking that she would want you to have some of it."

Eli shook his head. "Don't worry about me. I have some savings, just enough for me for a grubstake. This Depression ain't going to last forever."

Helen rose. She extended both of her hands across the desk while Eli grasped them and stood up.

"Thanks for everything, Eli. I'll see you at Lucy's funeral. If you should change your mind about the money—"

"I won't."

Helen turned slowly toward the door.

## 50

Helen's eyes welled up as she gazed at Lucy's casket. Besides the gravediggers and the Methodist pastor, only George Brewer and Eli Buchanan were present at the cemetery service. She felt the reassuring hold of George's hand as he tenderly rubbed her back. Helen cuddled closer to him and buried her face into his chest. She began to sob. In response, she could feel George's grip tighten. His embrace made her feel frail.

"We anticipate the day when spirit and body shall be united again at the coming of the Lord, and we find great comfort in ..." The voice of the minister droned on. His voice was merely secondary to the sorrow that burned in Helen's heart. She retreated from George's refuge and looked beyond the small group of mourners. Nearby the sight of the raw mound of earth marking Vincent's resting place pierced her heart. The pain she felt at hearing the news of losing him returned—it burned.

"Helen?" George whispered. Bewildered, she looked at him with vacant eyes. She regarded the small container full of dirt and a miniature shovel with puzzlement.

"Helen." He offered the receptacle of soil.

She freed herself of his embrace and took it with both hands before scooping out some of its contents to cast onto Lucy's casket. Eli took the container from her and, likewise, paid his respects.

The pastor followed by saying the final prayer. "Almighty God, as you once called your sister Lucy into this life, so now you have called her into everlasting life. We, therefore, commit Lucy to the elements in the hope of resurrection into eternal life. Through the promise of Our Lord Jesus Christ, we faithfully and victoriously give her to your blessed care. Amen."

Feeling her own sorrow ablaze within her, Helen looked at Eli, who stood alone, weeping. She went over to comfort him.

With trembling hands, he welcomed her with an embrace. She felt his chest heave in anguish while his tears mingled with her own against her cheek. In that brief moment, Helen bore Eli's pain.

Eli kissed her on her cheek before breaking free but took her hands in his. "Thank you for coming," he said softly. "I know it must have been difficult."

Helen closed her eyes in tender assent, opened them, then gave one final squeeze of her hands prior to leaving. With a suspended hand, Eli gave her one last wave.

Dr. George Brewer reached out and guided Helen to his car.

"Is there anything I can do for you, Helen?" he asked, holding the car door open for her.

She gazed at him with penetrating eyes. "George, do you love me?"

Helen saw, by his reaction, more surprise than agreement.

"I... I do love you, but we haven't talked about—"

"I'm sorry," she interrupted. "I shouldn't have put you on the spot like that." Helen turned away and raised herself onto the passenger seat.

George, appearing mystified by her comment, solemnly closed the door. When he reappeared on the driver's side and took his place behind the wheel, Helen said, "I didn't mean to say that. I guess I was wondering if your concern for me was motivated by love, let's say, a doctor caring for his patient?"

"Ah... I." George hopelessly stumbled for a response.

"I shouldn't have said anything. Please, George, ignore what I said. I'm dealing with a lot of emotions right now. Frankly, I'm afraid of being alone for the rest of my life. Vincent was my link to my past, as well as my future. I don't know how to cope with everything. I want to belong. Do you know what it is to belong?"

George nodded. "I do. I came here to find a purpose—someone to help. It wasn't just one person in Chandlers Bend that needed me—it was a community. So, when you asked me if I know what it's like to belong, I can honestly say that I do. If I was to consider leaving, I'm not certain I could. I'm an integral part of Chandlers Bend. I belong here."

Helen looked straight ahead while George started the car. "I'm tired," Helen said wistfully.

"Shall I take you home?"

"No, I don't have a home anymore. Take me to my house," Helen said despondently.

When Helen opened her front door, she felt the weight of an empty house. She wanted to shout that she was home, but she knew her words would not be met with a response. Unhurriedly, she went through the parlor and ascended the stairs to the second floor. Helen stopped outside Vincent's room. She knocked, as she always did before entering, then slowly opened the door.

## 51

E li left the cemetery and headed to his apartment. When he passed his landlord, Mrs. Larpin, she avoided his glance, acting as if he were invisible. Eli knew she had ample time to show up at Lucy's funeral. Her absence hurt.

Determined by retribution and regret, Eli collected the remnants of his ill-gotten effects and headed for his office. Once there, he immediately bundled the money into a tight parcel, searched his correspondence for an address, then proceeded to the Chandlers Bend's post office.

Located at the back of the Chandlers Bend's General Store, the post office was the paragon of bureaucratic neatness. Separated from the rest of the store by a partition of individual squares stood a wall of postal boxes, labeled with a number. In the heart of this governmental design was a caged window. Behind the bared opening, John Chandler busied himself with the task of overseeing the exchange of correspondence. He examined Eli with some curiosity.

"Good morning, Eli," John Chandler said with some hesitancy.

"John," Eli countered indifferently.

"I heard you buried Lucy Lareau today," Chandler muttered irreverently.

"Yeah," Eli snapped.

John Chandler did not look up but continued to leaf through several envelopes. "So, what brings you here today?"

"I want to mail this package."

Setting the mail aside, John Chandler approached the window. He studied the tightly wrapped package secured in bailing twine. "You don't have a return address on it. Aren't you afraid it may not make it to Hastings, Minnesota, and won't be able to be returned to you?"

"I'm sure it'll get there."

John Chandler removed the packet off the shelf and placed it on the scale. Following a meticulous adjustment of the slider on the beam, he said, "That'll be one dollar and twenty cents."

Eli laid the money on the sill and exited so quickly that he never heard the parting goodbye.

The street's of Chandlers Bend was busy with trade. People moved about freely, each with their interests, and Eli felt somewhat disconnected from them. It was an odd feeling for him to feel this way. With previous concern for their wellbeing gone, he now considered them strangers—he was now an alien in an unfamiliar land. Not only did he feel this way, but he also despised them and their uncaring attitude toward Lucy.

Eli mounted the Farmers & Mercantile Bank of Chandlers Bend's steps and caught a glimpse of Bill Larson going into his office.

Evelyn Ferris looked up from her teller's cage. "Good morning, Eli," she said in a more guarded manner than her usual exuberance.

"Good morning, Evelyn."

Evelyn leaned forward caringly and spoke softly. "Eli, I heard that Lucy was buried today. I am very sorry for your loss. Knowing your feelings for her, please accept my condolences."

Eli nodded. "Thanks, Evelyn."

Evelyn drew back. "So, what can I do for you today?" she asked delicately.

"I want to withdraw all my money."

"All of it?"

"Yep, all of it."

"I have to inform Mr. Larson. I'm sorry, Eli. He has to approve anything over five hundred dollars. "I'll only be a minute," Evelyn said and scurried off.

When she returned, Bill Larson was in tow.

"Eli," Bill said in acknowledgment and eyed him with curiosity. "Evelyn tells me that you want to withdraw all of your money. Something wrong with keeping it in our bank?"

"I have some expenses to take care of."

"Well, if it's money that you need, we—"

"Listen, Bill, I want my money, and that's it. I don't think I have to explain why."

Displaying the awkwardness of a reprimanded, Larson said, grudgingly, "Give him his money." He then turned hurriedly towards his office, slamming the door behind him.

Evelyn, forcing an apologetic smile, took Eli's bank deposit book and noted the amount. "I don't keep that much money in my drawer," she said and turned away toward the safe.

When Evelyn returned, and without further intercourse except to note the amount of withdrawal, she began to count out Eli's entire savings amount. "One thousand two hundred and fifty-four dollars," she said with finality as she placed the last dollar bill on the stack.

"Thanks, Evelyn," Eli said as he reached for the pile of bills. He added purposely, in a loud sonorous voice, "I'm sorry that you were caught in the middle of this." Intentionally loud in his remark, he knew his words would travel beyond Bill Larson's closed door.

She nodded uneasily and strained a smile as Eli turned to leave.

Outside the bank, Eli noticed Olive Perkins as she made her way through the Chandler Telegraph's front door. With a purposeful walk, he set his course after her. Once inside, he found Charlie Perkins in front of his linotype keyboard.

Charlie looked up. "Hi, Eli. I don't usually see you here unless there is some problem. And I'm guessin' there's a problem."

"Charlie, I just saw Olive come in here. I'd like to talk to her," he yelled over the noise of the linotype machine.

"Sure thing. She's on the loading dock." He made a sweeping motion with his hand toward the back of the office. "Go on, you know the way," he shouted, then resumed typing.

When Eli saw Olive, he detected some unease in her. "If you came here to talk about Vincent and Lucy, I had no—"

"I didn't come here for any of that business. You'll have to live with the consequences for the rest of your life."

Olive stared at him with hard eyes. "So, why are you here?" she barked.

"I came here to give you a scoop."

An obvious wave of curiosity replaced her uneasiness. "What kind of scoop?" she asked distrustfully.

Eli took a step in her direction. Instinctively, she moved back. He smiled. "I didn't come here to hurt you." He reached into his shirt's breast pocket.

Still looking warily at his actions, Eli saw her face switch to surprise as he produced his badge. He held it out to her, and with reluctance, she accepted. "Why are you giving me this?"

"Because I want you to be the first person to know that I'm leaving this damn town. This is your big scoop. Isn't this the stuff you live for? You don't give a shit about the people in Chandlers Bend, do you? It's all about the story. Right? You're nothing but a gossip who legitimizes your existence by calling yourself a reporter." Eli turned to leave. He paused and looked back at Olive. "And you can quote me," he said caustically before turning toward the door.

In the open air, Eli drew in a deep breath before going back to his rooming house. He gathered his belongings into a small suitcase and left without being spotted by Abagail Larpin or any other tenant. Near the front verandah, Eli snatched a cluster of red yarrow wildflowers and laid them on his car's passenger side, then headed to the cemetery.

Alone with his thoughts, Eli placed the bouquet on the fallow mound of Lucy's grave and reflected on what may have been. His ideas turned to tears before saying his final goodbye.

## 52

H elen was in the backyard, hanging laundry, when Eli pulled up the sidestreet, along the side of her house. With one hand securing a bedsheet with a clothespin, the other waved a greeting as he approached her. "I had to do something to keep my mind from brooding," she said. "Besides, I still have customers to take care of."

Eli took hold of one of the clothes poles that propped up the clothesline. His hand moved along with it as the wind caused it to sway. "You don't have to do this anymore," he said in mild rebuke.

"I don't know what to do," she answered unemotionally while continuing to hang laundry on the bobbing clothesline.

"Well, I've made up my mind. I'm leaving town today."

She paused and studied him as a teacher would a student who was about to recite his answer.

"I turned in my badge."

"Can't say I'm surprised," she said and threw a couple of clothes-pins into a half bushel wood basket that sat near her feet. A stiff breeze from the northwest billowed the sheets while her apron flapped uncontrolled. "Come into the house before you go."

"I really should get going, Helen."

"Just for a few minutes," she pleaded.

Eli shrugged. "Okay, but only for a couple of minutes."

Helen directed Eli to one of the kitchen chairs before she went to a cookie jar and pulled out a wad of money. "Here, I want you to have this," she said and placed the roll of cash in front of him.

Eli waved it off. "I don't want any money. It's all yours."

"I know, you said so when you found it in the suitcase. No, you take it. I insist. What's left is more than enough for me to start a new life."

"Have you decided where you'll go?"

"I have a cousin who lives in Minneapolis. I think I'll start there."

"What about your house?"

"Do you think someone is going to buy this place with its history? No, I'll lock her up and hope for the best, but I know what will happen. Some kid, with nothing better to do, will throw a rock at one of the windows. Soon, another will do the same. Before long, they'll break into my place and begin to steal things. Like vultures preying on a dead carcass rotting in a field, they'll pick away at its bones until little is left, except the deed to a house with a sordid past. When the taxes aren't paid, the house will go on the auction block."

Eli nodded. "I suppose you're right."

Helen's eyes grew thoughtful. "Eli, what do you expect to find in the Dakotas?"

Eli shifted in his chair. "The truth is, I don't expect to find anything. I only want to get lost. I want to find a town where my past doesn't follow me. I suspect that's the reason you want to leave, too."

Helen took the corner of her apron and dabbed at her moist eyes. "Trouble is, I don't know how to leave. How does one simply walk away from your life, Eli? It's easy for you because you're a man. For a woman alone in these uncertain times—it's hard and dangerous. That's why I'm going to go and live with my cousin and her husband for a while. But I just don't know how to make that first step. This here house isn't holding me—it's fear that's coiled around my legs."

"You just make up your mind and leave. It's that simple." Eli pushed back his chair and rose, leaving the money on the table.

Helen scooped up the cash and thrust it into Eli's chest. "Take it. You'll need it," she said, forcefully holding the money against him until he finally yielded.

He placed the money into his trouser's pocket and hugged her.

Helen returned the hug with a kiss on his cheek. "God be with you, Eli."

Eli nodded, his eyes welling up before turning toward the door to leave.

---

## 53

Nearly a week passed before Helen took Eli's advice to leave Chandlers Bend. With her bags already packed and sitting inside the front door, Helen made her final rounds. The house, buttoned-up tightly, was airless under a cloudless scorching August sky. Starting with the upper floor, she closed each room, beginning with her own, before moving to Lucy's old room. Turning to Vincent's already closed door, Helen knocked gently, then placed her palm tenderly against the wood as she would have stroked her son's face if he were present. "Goodbye," she whispered, then turned slowly away. Her legs unsteady, she walked downstairs.

With two suitcases firmly in her hands, Helen began the long walk to the train station. Her exodus, noted by a few of Chandlers Bend's residents who chanced to venture out under the August sun, was met with indifference. Only a nod or brief wave passed between them and without commentary. Along the way, Helen spotted the telltale signs of the curious as drapes fell back into place as she passed.

Struggling with her suitcases, she observed Bobby O'Dell as she ascended the set of steps to the railroad station. He sat peacefully on a wooden crate at the far end of the platform holding an open book on his lap. Looking up at her, he smiled and gave her a wave. She returned his smile.

As she began to grapple with the train depot's screendoor and its resilient spring, a waiting passenger got up from his perch to hold the door. "Good morning, ma'am. Allow me to assist you," he said.

Helen smiled briefly at the man and moved listlessly to the station master's window. She rested her arms on the arched window's ledge. "Good morning, Roger," she called out to get his attention as he chalked in times on his blackboard.

Roger turned toward her. "Well, this is a surprise. Don't recollect the last time I've seen you, Mrs. Spencer."

"It was years ago. Me and my boy—"

"You plan on catching the morning train to St. Paul?" he asked rudely.

His uncaring attitude put her off. Helen hesitated.

"Well?" he prodded curtly.

"Why, no. I'm going to Minneapolis."

Roger looked at the station's wall clock. "Should be here in about half an hour. Round trip?"

"No, one way," Helen said, almost choking on her answer.

He gave her an indifferent look, "Let's see... That'll be three dollars and sixty-two cents."

Money changed hands, and the ticket stamped—then without so much as a thank you or goodbye, Helen grabbed her bags and took a seat. She sat on the opposite side of the waiting room, facing the man who helped her. She briefly acknowledged him with her eyes then studied the backs of her worn hands. Occasionally, her meditative gaze drifted from her lap to the gaps of the scuffed floorboards, then back again to him only to repeat the cycle.

The station's clock loudly marked off the passage of time. With its annoying repetitive tick, a solitary fan rested on a shelf high over the stationmaster's protective wall. It fought against the determined muggy summer air, driving it momentarily aside with each fleeting swish. Flies, driven by heat or madness, fruitlessly assaulted the screendoor—their buzzing, in conflict with the fan and clock grated on Helen's nerves.

She examined the man again and returned his smile. She judged him to be in his mid-forties. He was clean-shaven, and by the case at his side, probably a salesman.

"I couldn't help but hear that you're going to Minneapolis, ma'am."

Helen nodded before unemotionally replying. "I have a sister there."

"Nice to have family in these trying times," he said. "Minneapolis is a lovely town, but everyone is having a hard time there as well."

"Is that where you live?" Helen asked hesitantly.

"No, ma'am. I go there quite often on business. I came up from Madison and spent the night in that hotel, back yonder." He pointed in the direction of the Bluff Side Hotel. "I'm only goin' as far as Red Wing."

"Your home?"

"I guess you could say so, but I don't spend a lot of time there. I work for the Red Wing Shoe Company that has just introduced a steel toe boot. Once I increase the demand in my territory, I'm expecting I won't have to travel as much."

"Steel-toed boots?"

He chuckled. "Yes, ma'am. Gonna prevent a lot of broken toes."

The anxiety of leaving Chandlers Bend eased up a bit, and Helen began to feel at ease. *This stranger knows nothing about me and treats me with total courtesy. I can't believe I'm actually leaving this town.*

In the distance, she heard two long train whistles followed by one short than another long blast.

"Appears like our train's coming," the man said as he rose off the bench. He approached Helen and extended his hand. "I'm sorry I didn't introduce myself. My name's Robert. Robert Wells. My friends call me Bob."

Helen accepted his hand. "My name is Helen Spencer, Mr. Wells. Pleased to make your acquaintance."

"Please, I don't mean to be forward, Mrs. Spencer, but may I have the pleasure of your company as far as Red Wing?"

"I suspect you are free to sit wherever you want, Mr. Wells. And it's Miss Spencer."

Robert Wells smiled uneasily. "May I give you a hand with that large suitcase?"

She nodded. "I would appreciate that, Mr. Wells."

Helen walked out onto the train station's platform while the salesman held the door for her.

"Okay, Miss Spencer, lead the way. I'll be right behind you."

The train appeared around the bend and tooted its warning signal again, only more penetratingly as it sluggishly chugged its way toward them. As it came to a stop, the train's whistle blew one long blast before releasing a cloud of steam. A conductor sprang from the passenger car's open door and placed a small stool at the foot of the stairwell.

"Stand back, please," the conductor said as he aided three men off the car. The oldest of the trio wore an old-fashioned bowler hat, while another wore a fedora. The third and last to get off the train wore a western-style hat and donned a U.S. Marshall's badge. The man with the bowler tipped his hat as he passed Helen.

Helen, feeling lightheaded, swayed slightly. The conductor was near enough to catch her by the arm and steadied her.

"Do you need a hand with that bag, ma'am?" the conductor asked as he held her.

"No, thank you. I'm fine," she said and moved up the set of steps.

The train conductor took her other large suitcase and stored it at the end of the car.

Helen felt the piercing stares of the curious as she strode down the passenger car's walkway in search of a place to sit.

"There's a spot over there, on your right, Miss Spencer," Mr. Wells called out from behind.

Helen was about to slide into the seat but paused and gestured. "Right now, I don't feel comfortable near the window, Mr. Wells."

"Are you sure? It is a very scenic ride to Red Wing."

"I'm certain. Perhaps later," Helen said and moved back to allow Mr. Wells' transit to the window seat.

She placed her small suitcase under her chair before sitting down. Within minutes, she felt the tug of the train, and they began to move forward.

Mr. Wells gazed outside, appearing absorbed in the outdoor scenery. "Every time I come through this area," he said wistfully, "I am amazed by the beauty of these bluffs." He pointed. "You're from around here, Miss Spencer. Do you know the name of that bluff?"

Helen didn't have to look. She knew. Staring straight ahead, she mumbled, "Chinamans Bluff," then leaned back into her seat and closed her eyes.

# ACKNOWLEDGMENTS

Polar Photography,
The Lady Lake Chapter of the Florida Writers Association, and
Eileen Malinger

Shutterstock Images 174645749 & 1383378260

# ABOUT THE AUTHOR

Christopher Malinger lives with his wife Eileen, in Central Florida. His works include, *The Object of Desire*, which appeared in *Journeys VII*; an Anthology of Award-Winning Short Stories, published in 2014. Also, he was a winner of the Florida Writers Association's Adult Collection, Volume 7, *The Sweet Scent of Spring; published in 2015*. And again in 2017, his short story, *Iggy*, was included in the 2017 Florida Writers Association's Adult Collection. In 2018 he was voted one of the top ten writers in the Florida Writers Association's Adult Collection, Volume 10, for his short story, *A Story Teller's Tale*. In 2019, the theme of the collection was, *Writers at Work* for which he won placement again for his story, *Inspiration*. At the time of this current printing of 2020, he was included in Volume 12, for his story *Jealousy*.

Other works include *Cat's Paw*, a fictional account of the bombing of British European Airline's Flight 284, published in 2016 and audiobook version in 2020. A collection of short stories, *Tales to Keep You Awake, The Back Roads of Terror*, and his novella, *The Wabele*, which won second place for general fiction in the 2017 annual Florida Writers Association Royal Palm Literary award's contest. In 2019, *Scrubbed* received the Silver Award for the unpublished (at the time) novella category.

He is a member of the Florida Writers Association.

www.ingramcontent.com/pod-product-compliance
Lightning Source LLC
Chambersburg PA
CBHW050512260626
47157CB00004B/1294